Mary Elizabeth Braddon

One Life, One Love

Vol. 3

Mary Elizabeth Braddon

One Life, One Love
Vol. 3

ISBN/EAN: 9783337049904

Printed in Europe, USA, Canada, Australia, Japan

Cover: Foto ©Andreas Hilbeck / pixelio.de

More available books at **www.hansebooks.com**

ONE LIFE, ONE LOVE

𝔄 𝔑𝔬𝔳𝔢𝔩

BY THE AUTHOR OF

"LADY AUDLEY'S SECRET," "VIXEN," "ISHMAEL,"
"THE DAY WILL COME"

ETC.

IN THREE VOLUMES

VOL. III.

LONDON

SIMPKIN, MARSHALL, HAMILTON, KENT & CO.

LIMITED

STATIONERS' HALL COURT

1890

LONDON:
PRINTED BY WILLIAM CLOWES AND SONS, LIMITED,
STAMFORD STREET AND CHARING CROSS.

CONTENTS OF VOL. III.

ONE LIFE, ONE LOVE.

CHAPTER I.

"ENOUGH THAT I CAN LIVE."

As Clara Arden anticipated, dinner was late that evening at River Lawn. It was nearly half-past eight when Mr. and Mrs. Arden and Daisy met in the drawing-room. The cook was angry, and the butler had been waiting for nearly half an hour to announce dinner.

"You are looking so pale and so tired, Ambrose," Mrs. Arden said, as they seated themselves in the light of the large central lamp, supplemented with clusters of wax candles, a light in which she could see the colour and expression of his face better than in the chastened lamplight of the drawing-room.

"I don't think that I am any more tired than usual," he answered. "You know what your fashionable physician said of me. You must not expect me to look particularly robust."

"He said that you were not to do much brain-work, Ambrose, and you have been doing nothing else since he saw you."

"Old habits are not so easily put off as doctors pretend to think. They tell the drunkard he must leave off brandy, and they tell the scholar he must live without books, with just the same admirable complacency, as if they were asking very little."

"I'm afraid we ought to leave Berkshire," pursued his wife, looking at him anxiously. "I am sure that you will be better away from your books."

"I shall be ready to leave my books when my own book is finished. I am nearing the end. When that is done I will go where you like."

"It is not where I like, but where you like," she said sadly. "I am happier here than any-where else."

"Then let us stay here—till the end of our lives. You know what Horace says, Daisy—a man may change his surroundings but not his mind."

"No, no, I am not selfish enough to keep you here," said Mrs. Arden, "when I see you dispirited and out of health. We will go back to London; we will go to Italy; anywhere."

There was a silence after this, Daisy being more thoughtful than usual, and not offering any diversion by the girlish prattle with which she usually brightened the meal, whether her heart was light or heavy. No word had yet been spoken about Cyril's absence. The butler had quietly removed the cover laid for him, and the chair in which he was to have sat; but nobody mentioned his name till nearly the end of the meal, when Clara said rather nervously—

"Cyril is dining out, I suppose?"

"He has gone to London," Ambrose Arden answered quietly. "He is not coming back to-night."

Clara looked at him wonderingly as he answered. Had Cyril told his father that his engagement was at an end? She could hardly believe that her husband would have taken the blow so calmly. It was left for her, she thought, to tell him of his disappointment.

Daisy slipped away to her own den as soon as she was free to leave the dining-room, and Mrs. Arden entered the drawing-room alone, and sat there waiting anxiously for her husband to rejoin her. It was very seldom that he lingered in the dining-room after his wife left him, but this evening he was sitting in an abstracted mood at his end of the table, and did not stir when mother and daughter rose and went away. It was perhaps the first time that he had ever allowed his wife to open that door for herself when he was in the room. Absent-minded and dreamy by temperament, he had yet rarely failed in courtesy to the woman who was to him this world's one woman.

He sat with his head bent over the empty dessert-plate, and the untouched glass of claret which the butler had filled. He sat brooding in the lamplight for nearly half an hour; and then, with a deep-drawn sigh, he rose slowly, and went to the drawing-room, where his wife was sitting by an open window looking out at the moonlit water, very sad at heart.

He went over to her and seated himself by her side.

"Cyril is gone from us for good, Clara," he said. "I suppose you know that?"

"I know that all is over between him and Daisy; but I thought you did not know. I feared you would not be able to take the blow so quietly, knowing how pleased you were at their engagement."

"I was pleased because it was a link that drew me nearer to you. It was of *our* union I thought, not theirs. Nothing can touch me, Clara, while I have you."

"Did he tell you why he and Daisy had made up their minds to part?"

"Yes, he told me his reasons."

"And hers. You will blame my daughter for fickleness, I fear, Ambrose."

"Blame her! blame Daisy! Your daughter—

and my pupil. Why, she was the bond between us years ago, when I was but the stranger within your gates. My love for your daughter is second only to my love for you."

His wife took up his hand and kissed it, in a rapture of grateful affection.

"How good you are to us, Ambrose!" she said softly. "Harsh words never fall from your lips. If I could only see you happy, my heart would be full of content."

"I am happy, Clara, happy in having won my heart's desire. What can a man have in this world more than that—the one desire of his life, the boon for which he has waited and longed through years of patient, silent hope? If there is happiness upon earth I have attained it."

"I believe your metaphysicians teach you that there is no such thing as happiness."

"Oh, they only preach the gospel of doubt. The whole science of metaphysics consists in the questioning spirit, which analyzes everything, without arriving at any definite conclusion about anything."

"Poor Cyril!" sighed Clara, after a pause of contemplative silence, which seemed in harmony with the stillness of the summer night and the beauty of the moonlit landscape, garden and river, meadow and woodland, and dark church tower. "Poor Cyril!" she repeated. "It seems so sad for him to leave us, to go out into the world as a wanderer; and yet it would be impossible for our old life to go on, now that he has broken with Daisy."

"No, the old life would not be possible. It belongs to the past already. Did he tell Daisy where he was going?"

"To Australia, he said. He consulted with you as to his destination, no doubt."

"No; he told me he should go away; but he did not enter upon his plans."

"Poor fellow! He was very unhappy, I fear."

"He did not confide his sorrows to me. He had made up his mind; and it was not for me to try to change his resolution."

His whole manner altered as he spoke of his son. There was a hardness in his tone that surprised and grieved his wife, who a minute before had done him homage as the most admirable of men. His manner in speaking of her daughter had expressed the utmost tenderness. The tone in which he spoke of his own son was stern almost to vindictiveness. Clara feared there had been a quarrel between father and son, and that Ambrose Arden had resented the cancelment of Daisy's engagement with an unjust wrath.

"You must not be angry with Cyril," she said softly. "I fear that it is Daisy's fickleness that is the beginning and end of our disappointment. She owned as much to me, poor child. She gave her promise too lightly, and repented almost as soon as it was given, although she had not the courage to confess her mistake."

"Well, we will say it is Daisy's fault, or that both are fickle. There are no hearts broken, I believe. Cyril goes out into the world, a stranger to us henceforward."

"Not a stranger, Ambrose. Your son will always be dear to us both."

"He will be in Australia, where our love or our indifference cannot touch him."

There was a bitterness in his tone which warned Clara to pursue the subject no further. She could not doubt after this that there had been a breach between father and son—that these two who had been so fond of each other and so proud of each other hitherto had parted ill friends. And it was all Daisy's doing, poor little feather-headed Daisy! who should have been a bond of union, but had become the occasion of severance.

Clara Arden felt weighed down by inexpressible sadness as she sat looking out into the moonlit garden, that garden which she and her first lover had found a wilderness, and which he had made into a paradise for her sake. It was her girlish admiration of that old garden by the river which had made Robert Hatrell eager to possess the place. He had laid it at her feet, as if it were a bunch of roses, never counting the cost of anything which pleased her. Had it been ten times as costly a place he would have bought it for her.

His image was with her to-night more vividly than it had been for a long time. It was as if he himself were at hand, in all the warmth and vigour of life, and that she had but to stretch out her arms to beckon him to her. And, oh, with what a heart-sickness of longing and regret she turned towards that idolized image! Face to face with the inexplicable gloom of Ambrose Arden's temper, she recalled her first husband's happy nature, his joyous outlook, and keen delight in life. With him her days had seemed one perpetual holiday. If she ever complained it had been because that energetic temperament took life and its enjoyments at a faster pace than suited her own reposeful temper. But how bright, how gay those days had been; how frank and open her companion's face; how expansive his speech and manner! He had never hidden a care from her. Were his thoughts light or heavy she shared them, and knew every desire of her heart.

But in this man, this cherished friend of many years, she had discovered mysteries. He had griefs which he would not share with her. He was angry with his only son; they had parted within a few hours, perhaps for all this life; and he would tell her nothing of the cause of their parting, he invited no sympathy. He sat by her side in melancholy silence, and she felt the burden of unhappiness which she was not allowed to share.

"If he would only talk of his trouble, if he would only let me comfort him, I should be twice as good a wife," she thought despondently. "It is not my fault if our lives are growing farther apart."

After this night an emotionless monotony marked Clara Arden's days in the house where her early married life had been so full of happiness, and where her one great sorrow, the sorrow of a lifetime, had come upon her. The idea of going on the Continent for the autumn was not carried out. The scholar's book absorbed him wholly in the waning of the year, and he preferred the quiet of River Lawn to the glory of the Italian Lakes, or the art-treasures of Florence.

He spent a good many hours of every day in his old cottage-study, while his wife and her daughter lived very much as they had lived in Mrs. Hatrell's widowhood.

"Your second marriage and my engagement to Cyril seem almost a dream, mother, when you and I are sitting here alone together, and Uncle Ambrose is poring over his books on the other side of the road," said Daisy, as she sat at her mother's feet in the morning-room, pretending to read Lecky's "England in the Eighteenth Century," but looking up every now and then to talk. "I call him quite a perfect husband in his way —never interfering with our plans, never grumbling at his dinner, always courteous and kind and ready to do what we like."

"Yes, he is all goodness to us," answered her mother, "and one would have nothing left to wish for if he were only happy."

"I dare say he *is* happy—in his way, mother— his calm, philosophical way, which used to soothe and tame me in my rebellious fits when I was a child. He was always the same, don't you know?

Tranquil and rather mysterious—like deep still water: like Lake Leman, whose depth one would never suspect if one did not see the mountains upside down in the water—suggesting by their delusive shadows the real depth below. Rely upon it, Uncle Ambrose has all he cares for in this world, having you and his books, and you give yourself groundless trouble when you are anxious about him."

Her mother sighed, but did not answer. She had watched her husband's face with a new anxiety ever since Cyril's departure; and she had seen the lines deepen, and the melancholy droop of the firm lips grow more marked.

No one at River Lawn knew anything about Cyril's whereabouts, unless it was his father. He had left Lamford within a few hours of his interview with Daisy, taking with him only a single portmanteau, as Beatrice Reardon informed her friend, this young lady having a knack of meeting every fly that ever entered or departed from the village.

" It's no use telling me you haven't quarrelled,"

protested Beatrice, when Daisy denied any ill-feeling between Cyril and herself. "I saw the poor fellow's white face as he drove by, acknowledging my bow in the most distracted manner, and I never saw such a change in any man. A few hours before he had been the gayest of us all on the tennis lawn, and now he looked positively like his own ghost. You must have had a dreadful row, Daisy."

"We had no row, as you call it. We only agreed that it was better for us to part."

"Poor Cyril! I had no idea he was so desperately in love with you. He used to take things so very easily," remarked Beatrice, with all the freedom of friendship. "Of course I always suspected you of not caring a straw for him. You were not the least like an engaged girl. You didn't spoon him a little bit."

Daisy shuddered. She was one of the few girls who are revolted by such forms of speech as prevail in some girlish circles. Miss Reardon affected a fast and slangy manner as a kind of perpetual protest against the dulness and monotony of her life in a Berkshire village. She wanted everybody to understand that there was nothing rustic or pastoral about her mind or her manners.

This was all that Daisy or her mother heard about Cyril's departure. He had gone to his chambers most likely, where he could prepare at his leisure for that long voyage of which he had talked. The greater part of his possessions, his books and guns, and sporting tackle of all kinds were in the Albany. He had his own man to pack for him, and accompany him to a new world, if he was so minded.

CHAPTER II.

DAISY'S DIARY.

How peacefully the days have slipped by since
poor Cyril went away! I find myself thinking of
him and writing of him as " Poor Cyril!" which
is really an impertinence, and I dare say by this
time he is perfectly happy, and has fallen in love
with some magnificent Australian girl, a higher
order of being, like the Gy in the Coming Race
—a powerfully built creature who can ride buck-
jumpers, and camp out in the bush, without fear
of consequences. I fear I have very narrow and
insular ideas about Australia, which I can only
picture to myself as one vast jungle, tempered
with convict settlements.

Cyril is happy no doubt by this time, sad as
he looked on that day of sudden parting; so I
may allow myself to feel happy, with an easy

conscience. I should be perfectly happy if it were not for the change in Uncle Ambrose, who has evidently some secret grief, some corroding care which he will not lighten by sharing it with his wife. I can but fear that mother was right in her foreboding, and that he has taken the cancelment of Cyril's engagement sorely to heart. It is his love for mother which is wounded. He wanted a perfect union, that we should be one household, bound by every tie that can make a family circle indivisible. It must be very hard for him too to know that his son, his only child, has been self-banished from his home and his native country.

If my fickleness alone had been to blame; if Cyril had found out my foolish secret, and that the man who was nothing to me was a great deal nearer my heart than my plighted husband; if he had broken with me on this account, my conscience would hardly have been as easy as it is. But I have at least the comfort of knowing that Cyril had some weighty reason upon his own side for parting from me—and that I am not actually to blame for the existing state of thin s. It was he who took the initiative. It was he who said, " All is over between us."

I have left off puzzling myself with idle speculations about his motive. Whatever his reason may have been, I feel assured that it was very serious and entirely convincing to his own mind —that he obeyed what to him was a stern necessity. I can but be grateful to Providence that has released me from a bond that could not have brought real happiness to either Cyril or me; and, looking back now at the past, I feel how cowardly I was in not telling him the truth about my own feelings. *He* was no coward. When the hour came in which he felt he ought to break with me, there was no hesitation or wavering on his side; and yet I believe he loved me better in that parting hour than he had ever loved me in his life before. Poor Cyril—old friend and playfellow! I hope his Australian wife will be kind and true, and that his life in that far world may be full of all good things : gold in monster nuggets, sheep in mighty flocks, horses that are not buck-jumpers, woods of eucalyptus, groves of mimosa, birds of vivid plumage, and the most perfect thing in bungalows.

I am really very sad about Uncle Ambrose. I think he fights against the gloom that gathers round him as a strong man stricken in the prime of life by some insidious malady might fight against disease: and yet the gloom deepens. With him low spirits seem actually a disease; and I tremble and turn cold sometimes at the thought that his depression may forebode some mental malady which may darken all our days. My mother seldom, if ever, sees him as I see him when she is not present. When she is with him I know that he makes a stupendous effort to appear cheerful, to seem interested in the things she loves; but when she leaves him the mask drops, and I see him as he really is—a man weighed down by deep-rooted melancholy.

I have talked to him of the books I used to read with him, the low-spirited school of metaphysicians, and of Heine, who saw all things with the saddened eyes of a man whose life was like

Pope's, a "long disease." We have talked of theology, and I have discovered the hopelessness of his creed—that for him there is nothing beyond this life of ours, this poor brief life, in which there are so many chances of being miserable against a single chance of being happy. No, for him there is no beyond—for him the dead are verily dead.

I told him yesterday that I believe not only in a world where we shall meet our loved and lost, and know them again, and live with them again in a better and loftier state of being; but that I also believe in the influence of our beloved dead upon our thoughts and actions, even while we are on this side of the veil that parts flesh and spirit.

"That influence is only memory," he said; "it has no other source than your own mind—moved by your own loving heart."

I told him that it was something more than memory—something independent of my own mind or my own heart—an influence that flashed upon me when least I expected it—sudden, mysterious, full of suggestions of another world.

I told him that there were moments in which I could feel that my father was with me, that he was loving and pitying me in my weakness as a woman, just as he used to pity me when I was a foolish child.

" A delusion, Daisy," he said—" a delusion like the rest of our dreams. Science has made an end of all such deceptions. The belief in a spirit-world was only possible while mankind remained densely ignorant of the world of sense."

" I know now why you grow sadder as life goes on," I said. " It must be so hard to feel that you are treading a path that only leads to a dead wall; that there is no door in the great cruel wall, no beyond. Thank God, to me it is harder to believe in extinction than in a world to come — a chain of worlds, if you will — a gradual ascent from this life with all its sin and misery, to the highest form of life conceivable. The most elaborate of those systems which you call superstitions seems simpler and easier for my understanding than the barren creed of the materialist."

"That is because you are young, Daisy, and full of enthusiasm, and because you know very little of the world in which you are one happy atom—a joyous mote dancing in the sunshine. You think life is the gift of a beneficent Creator, who holds in reserve future lives, fairer than this, for those who believe in Him and obey Him. That pretty creed comes naturally enough to you who know life only at River Lawn and in Grosvenor Square. But go and look at life in Whitechapel; put yourself into the skin of the women you will see there, and then ask yourself about the beneficent Creator, the Eternal Wisdom, who has made man in His own image. Your rose-water theories would hardly be strong enough to stand that atmosphere. Bradlaugh's vitriol better suits the district."

I told him that it was an old, old argument that because there was so much misery in the world He that made it could not be a just God; or rather that there could be no directing mind above the universe, only unreasoning matter working out its own destiny according to material and immutable laws; that the God who could be moved to pity was the God of children and visionaries only.

"You talk to me as if there had been no misery in *my* life," I said. "Do you forget what it was to me, in my happy childhood, to see the father I loved go out of this house one morning, and never to see him again? Do you forget what it was to me a year ago to discover the horror of his death? If I could rebel against the Power to which I have prayed ever since I knew what prayer meant, I should have rebelled then."

I could not go on for the sobs that choked me at the thought of my father's cruel death. Uncle Ambrose melted in a moment, and took me in his arms, just as he would have done years ago in one of my childish troubles, and pressed his lips upon my forehead with a kiss that seemed like a blessing.

"Believe, my dearest," he said; "keep always that unquestioning faith which is the gift of the pure in spirit. It is a second sight, Daisy. It

is a sixth sense. It is given to the chosen few,
God's very elect. To them it is given to conceive and understand the unseen. They are
the children of light. Be always of that happy
race, Daisy. My reason has nothing to offer in
exchange for your clairvoyance. Remember
always that if I could not help you to believe
—if I could not enter with you into the holy of
holies, I never taught you to doubt."

"No, no. I have only known lately that you
yourself were without the hope that has sustained
mother and me in our dark hours."

He told me that I must not talk of dark
hours—that for me life was to be all sunshine;
and then, for the first time, he spoke of his
disappointment about Cyril and me—touching
on the subject very lightly, and, indeed, not
mentioning his son's name.

"A little hint of your mother's has helped me
to guess your secret, Daisy," he said, "and I love
you too well to blame your inconstancy. Your
mother and I both think that Mr. Florestan had
something to do with the change in your sentiments."

"Something to do with my finding out the truth about my own heart," I said, "and the nature of my mistake. I did not love Cyril less after I had seen Mr. Florestan, and found out somehow that he cared for me. But I knew all at once that my love for Cyril had never been the kind of love that would make me his happy wife. I found out that he could never be more to me than a dear and valued friend—never so much to me as you have been. He could never be the first; and one's husband ought to be the first in one's heart and mind, ought he not, Uncle Ambrose, as mother's husband was?"

I felt so sorry for my thoughtless words when I saw him wince at the mention of my father's name. It was such a heartless thing to say— as if *he* were something less than a husband, as if *he* hardly counted in my mother's life. I hung my head, deeply ashamed of myself, but feeling that any attempt to unsay what I had said would only make matters worse. And then again words cannot alter the truth. He knows that my mother has never loved him as she

loved her cherished dead; that the mere mention
of my father's name can move a deeper feeling
in her than all her second husband's adoring
tenderness.

There was an awkward silence, and then
Uncle Ambrose went on gravely and quietly,
with infinite kindness—

"I want my pupil and adopted daughter to be
happy, even if she cannot be bound any nearer
to me by a new tie. Don't be afraid to trust me,
Daisy. Remember I was your first friend—
after your father and mother, and that you used
to tell me all your thoughts and fancies. Try
to be as frank to-day as you were in those happy
hours when your doll used to sit in your lap and
share your history-lesson. You have some reason
to believe that Mr. Florestan cares for you?"

"He told me so one day," I faltered. "I was
alone in the summer-house in the shrubbery,
alone with my books, intending to spend a
studious morning. Mr. Florestan found me
there, and sat down and began to talk to me;
and before I knew what was coming he told me

that he was very fond of me, and that he was
sure I did not care quite so much as I ought
to care for Cyril; and he asked me to cancel my
engagement and marry him. I was very angry,
and I told him that he had no right to form
any such opinion about my sentiments, and that
nothing would induce me to break my promise to
Cyril."

"Yet you *did* break your promise, very soon
afterwards. How did you come to change your
mind so speedily?"

This was a searching question, and I felt
that I was on dangerous ground. Cyril told me
to let people suppose that I had broken our
engagement; and to tell the truth would be to
touch upon his secret, which he may have
wished to keep from his father's knowledge.

"Oh, the cancelment of our engagement arose
on the spur of the moment," I replied carelessly.
"Cyril and I were of one opinion."

"That is enough, child," Uncle Ambrose
answered kindly; "if Florestan is the chosen
man, I think he ought to be informed of what

has happened, and that the lady he loves is
free."

"Oh no, no, no, no!" I cried, in a great fright.
"He musn't be told anything. · Why, that would
be like putting me up to auction. If he really
cares for me his love will keep. If he rushes
off to propose to somebody else—as I have heard
of young men doing—that will only prove that
his love wasn't worth having. Let him wait, and
find out for himself that I am not going to marry
Cyril."

"What an arrogant young person you are!
But I suppose you must have your own way,"
said Uncle Ambrose; "only remember, Daisy,
that I want to see you happily married to the
man of your choice before I die. I want to be
sure that I have done all for your happiness
that your own father could have done had he
lived to bless you on your wedding day."

The deep grave tones of his voice, the solemn
expression of his eyes as he turned them upon
me, made my heart thrill with love and
reverence. Yes, he is a good man, a man in

whose character I have never discovered fault
or flaw.

"You are not going to leave us for many a
year to come," I said. "Indeed, indeed there is
no reason that my marriage should be hurried
on."

"Yes, Daisy, there is need. I want to see you
happy. I want, when I lie down on my bed for
the last time and turn my face to the wall, to
be able to say to myself, 'At least my little
friend Daisy is happy; I have been her friend
from the hour she learnt to read at my knees
until the hour I gave her to the husband of her
choice. No father upon this earth could have
been more careful of his daughter's happiness
than I have been of hers.' Perhaps in the last
hours, when mind and senses grow dim, I may
forget that my little pupil ever grew up to
womanhood; I may think of you as a child still,
flitting about the garden with streaming hair.
I may see you thus in the dim past, and not
recognize the real Daisy when she stands beside
my bed and looks at me with pitying eyes."

These sad forebodings made me cry; and I kissed Uncle Ambrose and tried to comfort him, and felt as fond of him as I used to be when I was a child. I was glad that the old feeling came back, for of late, though I know always that he is my best friend, after my mother, we seem to have been growing further apart; and I have had a curious sense of apprehension when I have been in his company, as if there were some evil influence for me lurking under the gloomy cloud which has darkened his life. To-day I felt only a great pity and a great love, the old confidence and affection which used to fill my heart when I ran across the lawn of a morning to meet him as he came in at the gate. I pitied him, because I began to fear that the shadow that rests upon him is the shadow of a closing life, and that it is some deep-rooted malady which makes him so joyless amidst our happy surroundings. I fear that his own forebodings may be too surely realized, and that he will never see the quiet, long-spun-out days of a good old age. This thought made me very melancholy after this serious interview; yet it was a great relief to find that he did not disapprove of Mr. Florestan as a lover for me. Who knows? Mr. Florestan may be as fickle as the inconstant moon; and all that impulsive nonsense of his in the arbour may be utterly forgotten on his part, though I remember every syllable. I wonder what he is doing in Scotland. I think he ought to have shot everything shootable in Argyleshire by this time.

CHAPTER III.

WHERE THE GOLD CAME FROM.

DON PEDRO PEREZ, more commonly spoken of in
the Parisian world as le vieux Perez, or Perez
Peru, was one of the best-known men in Paris;
and yet he but rarely appeared in those places
where the world of Paris most loves to con-
gregate. In the haunts of pleasure he was
almost a stranger. He hung about the side
scenes of no Boulevard Theatre; he frequented
not the racecourses of Longchamps or Auteuil.
He sat late at his club, playing whist; but the
club was quiet, and altogether out of the movement; and he was an unknown figure at those
more fashionable clubs where fortunes are lost at
baccarat. But there was one place where Señor
Perez reigned supreme, where his name was a
word of fear, his countenance an augury of gain

or loss to thousands. That place was the Bourse.
There Pedro Perez was as a king among his
fellow-men.

He was a Spaniard by birth, though he had
lived nearly half a century in Paris, or rather
had oscillated between Paris and Madrid during
that period. He dealt only in Spanish-American
securities. That line was his speciality. There
was not the most insignificant railway between
the southernmost point of Patagonia and the
mouth of the Amazon, between Buenos Ayres
and Quito; there was not a silver, diamond, or
copper mine within all that vast and varied
expanse of territory; there was not a water company or an irrigation company or a company for
making patent guano out of surplus paving-
stones, the history and vicissitudes, the exact
value or non-value of which Pedro Perez did not
know by heart. That withered old finger of his
had been in almost every financial pie which had
been cooked upon that southern continent. He
had been in at the death of more schemes than
he could have counted in a business morning. In

the earlier stage of his career, before he was rich enough to eschew barefaced fraud, he had been in his own person chairman, board of directors, and advising engineer of more than one railway which never reached a more tangible form of existence than paper and print. Many a scheme had lived, faded, and expired within the limits of a prospectus, while Perez swept the money of the shareholders into his own capacious pocket.

Don Pedro had been only a *coulissier* in those days; but with the progress of time and the suppression of the privileges of those financial sharpshooters—the guerilla band of the noble army of speculators—the Spaniard had put on that electro-plate surface of honesty which very often passes as genuine metal in the world of speculation. Investors followed him and confided in him because of his reputation for acumen and good luck, rather than because they believed that the Pedro Perez of to-day was altogether a different character from that Perez of thirty years ago about whom such queer stories were current.

He had been given the sobriquet of Perez Peru

because he was considered as deep and as rich as
the deepest mine in that vast Republic, and
perhaps partly because his complexion had a
tinge of that copper ore in which he had dealt so
largely. As Perez Peru he was talked about
respectfully even by the Tritons of the Bourse,
and watched closely by the eager-eyed Minnows
of that great mill, in which money and honour
are ground into dust and ashes, and dust and
ashes are ground back again into gold and good
name.

The first ten years of Perez Peru's financial
career had been years of struggle and petty
fraud. Petty fraud had failed to make him rich,
and timid speculation had only served to keep
him like Mahomet's coffin in a middle distance
between the heaven of wealth and the hell of
poverty. Then came his heroic period, which
was short and sharp, bolder speculation and
more uncompromising chicanery. Five years of
this hazardous adventure, in which he escaped
the galleys only by the skin of his teeth, made
him a capitalist; and fifteen years as a *coulissier*

had educated him in the deepest secrets of
finance. There was not a trick of the Stock
Exchange which Perez Peru had not at his fingers'
ends. He could stand idle, with his back
against a stone pillar, and with his crafty
southern eyes looking farther into futurity than
any other eyes in that crowded building. All
that he touched after this period seemed to turn
to gold. It turned to dross afterwards, perhaps ;
but not till Señor Perez had passed it on to
somebody else. He was never known to buy too
soon or to hold too long. In a word, he was
financial wisdom personified.

In all the monotonous years in which the
Stock Exchange was his only temple, the share
list his only Bible, Pedro Perez had lived with
an almost Spartan simplicity; not because he
begrudged himself the cost of luxurious living,
for personal expenditure, however profuse, would
have hardly made a perceptible impression upon
his income. He spent little because he cared for
making money and did not care for spending it.
He had lived in the same house in the Rue

Vivienne for the forty years of his Parisian life.
The house was within a hundred yards of the
Place de la Bourse, and it suited him.   The only
difference that he had made in those forty years
was to descend gradually from the scanty
seclusion of a single garret to the space and
comfort of the entire first floor.   He had break-
fasted at the Restaurant Champeaux during the
greater part of the last thirty years.   In his
decade of probation he had fed only in his attic,
or in some cheap restaurant on the Rive Gauche,
where he wandered in the cool of the evening,
thoughtful and solitary even before his thirtieth
year.   The   man   was   the   financial   instinct
incarnate.   The passion for abstract mathematics
which possesses some brains, in his took the more
vulgar form of money-getting; but the mathe-
matical genius was there to a high degree, and
some of his combinations were worthy of Newton
or Laplace.

For five and thirty years of his Parisian career
Pedro Perez had never been found guilty of a
caprice.   He was closely observed, as the repre-

sentative of great wealth always is observed, in
an age which has Mammon for its master-devil;
but he had never been surprised in any of those
follies which sometimes diversify the lives of the
wisest men. He had come to be looked upon as
a money-making machine, inexorable as steel and
adamant, working always in the same grooves,
relentless, unvarying; when all at once the report
was circulated that Perez Peru had come back
from Madrid with a "harem," and for more than
nine days, Perez Peru's harem was the standing
joke in the cafés where the Bourse is paramount.
Perez Peru's harem was the subject of a caricature
in the most audacious of the little journals of
Paris. Perez Peru's harem was the theme of a
comic song, almost as popular as the later
" Gendre de M. Grévy."

The harem upon closer inquiry was found to
consist of three women whom Perez had established
in a second floor in the Rue St. Guillaume. A
mother and daughter, both handsome, the
daughter eminently so; a cousin, plain and dowdy,
or, if not absolutely plain, faded and elderly.

The three women were seen one night in a box at the opera, the young beauty resplendent in amber satin and diamonds. Every lorgnette was turned to that box, and for the next three days all Paris talked of the dark beauty with the diamonds.

"She was wearing the wealth of Peru upon her neck and arms," said the *boursicotiers* and their following.

After this Dolores was rarely visible to the eye of all Paris. If she went to a theatre or an opera, and she was but seldom allowed that privilege, she was made to sit deep in shadow, as closely curtained from the public gaze as if she had been the Pearl of Istamboul, chief light of some jealous Pasha's harem.

Her story had but few elements of mystery, albeit her secluded life gave a flavour of the mysterious to her personality. She had been bargained for by Pedro Perez as sordidly as any Eastern slave that was ever sold in a public market-place. The girl and her mother had been living in poverty, in one of the obscurest quarters of Madrid, a region where the Cholera fiend and the Fever fiend find their choicest pasturage, where the reaper Death gathers his richest harvest. They had arrived in Madrid some years before with an appearance of ample means, and for a year or two Madame Quijada had occupied an apartment in a fashionable quarter, and had shown herself daily on the Prado, well-dressed, observed, and admired. She was taken to be an adventuress and a free lance; but no one troubled himself about her antecedents. The police had an eye upon her for the first few months, but could find nothing suspicious in her manner of life. Dolores was at a convent during the five or six years in which she grew from child-hood to girlhood. It was the best educational establishment in the neighbourhood of Madrid, and as the mother's funds got low she pinched herself in order to provide for her daughter's board and education with the good nuns, who, albeit simplicity itself, had a talent for making out a bill of extra charges, over and above the somewhat heavy *pension*.

Madame Quijada was not alone during these years of her daughter's education. Shortly after her arrival in the Spanish capital she was joined by a niece, who from that time shared her fortunes, good or bad. The niece was introduced to Madame Quijada's acquaintances as Louise Marcet, and she was said to have but recently recovered from a brain fever, which had seriously affected her mind and memory. Her aunt told her friends in confidence that this orphan niece of hers had been disappointed in love, and that her illness had been the outcome of her disappointment. However true this may have been, it was beyond question that a more miserable-looking woman than Louise Marcet at this period could hardly be found on this planet, where if people sometimes take their pleasures sadly they very often take their griefs gaily.

The time came when the widow's cruse would hold out no longer, and when it became necessary to withdraw Dolores from the fashionable convent. The good nuns affected a holy simplicity in their accounts, and they gave no credit.

Dolores was now eighteen, beautiful, carefully educated, fairly accomplished. She went from the pure atmosphere and perfect comfort of a well-organized educational establishment to a shabby lodging in a sordid quarter. She went from all the refinements of life to all that is ugliest in the domain of Poverty. The change was a shock which youthful selfishness felt keenly. Perhaps Madame Quijada was not sorry that her daughter suffered from the misery of her surroundings. It might prepare her mind for the crisis to which her mother looked forward.

Pedro Perez was almost as well known in Madrid as he was in Paris; and he was perhaps even more profoundly reverenced in' the less wealthy capital. Madame Quijada had contrived to force herself upon his notice, but she had approached him with a modesty which flattered his self-esteem. She had besought his counsel and assistance in certain little investments, so small in amount that the great financier was provoked to smile—he who so rarely smiled—at her simplicity. Such small investments had been his stepping-stones to fortune—such simple creatures as this shabby-genteel widow had put their little savings into those rotten enterprises of which Pedro Perez had been both the dazzling Alpha and the dark Omega. It was said in Paris that if you could squeeze Perez Peru's gold hard enough, blood would come out of it, by a lesser miracle than the squeezing of the blood of Christian martyrs out of the earth-floor of Nero's amphitheatre— the blood of broken-hearted widows, and starving orphans, the blood of the swindler's dupes.

The widow's tongue was soft and insinuating, and for almost the first time in his life Perez was moved to a benevolent action. He lent this simple lady fifty louis to invest in an Argentine Railway—lent fifty louis without security and without interest—but on second thoughts he insisted upon holding the scrip.

"Women are so shortsighted," he said, after making this condition, "you would be selling at the first rise. These shares are worth holding."

Madame Quijada was in sore need of fifty louis,

but it aided a certain plan of hers that Señor
Perez should hold the stock. It gave her a right
of approach to him. His image had dwelt in her
mind ever since she came to Spain, as the image
of wealth incarnate. She had dreamed her dream
about this rich lonely old man; and the hour for
the realization of that dream was at hand.

She wrote him a piteous letter about a fortnight
after Dolores left the convent, telling him she
was too ill to leave her wretched home, and she
was in want of money. She believed that the
dividend upon her Argentines was nearly due.
It would only amount, she supposed, to a couple
of louis, but forty francs would save her and
hers from starvation. She had now three mouths
to fill. Her daughter had been withdrawn from
the convent where she had grown up, and was
sharing the discomforts of her wretched lodging.

Pedro Perez was not given to acts of charity,
and was not in the habit of caring whether his
fellow-creatures dined or starved; but Madame
Quijada had contrived to impress him with the
idea that she was a remarkably clever woman,

and that the world would be the poorer for her loss. She had flattered him with such subtle comprehension of his character that he, who had been the mark of abject flattery for a quarter of a century, found himself listening with a pleased ear to this gifted woman's enthusiastic laudation of his talents as a financier, and of that latent genius which would have made him greater as a politician or a diplomatist than he had ever been on the Stock Exchange.

Had the flatterer been old and ugly, even feminine subtlety might have failed to win his ear; but Madame Quijada was still handsome and still young enough to seem attractive in the eyes of a man who had passed his sixtieth birthday. He was not in love with her; but he thought her a remarkably attractive woman, and instead of sending her fifty francs by his servant, he went himself to see in what kind of a den so much ability had found shelter.

He went, saw Dolores in all the splendour of her fresh young beauty, and was conquered. He had never known what it was to feel his heart

beat quicker at the sight of a woman's face till
he saw Madame Quijada's daughter. He was
subjugated at once and for ever. His instinct
urged him to make as hard a bargain as he
could with the girl's mother; but the settlement
to which he finally consented was more than
princely. Princes are seldom so generous. Had
Madame Quijada insisted upon his sacrificing his
last penny he would have done it sooner than
lose the woman he loved. Had she insisted upon
his marrying her daughter he would have done
it. Indeed, the chief consideration that prevented
his offering to make Dolores his wife was his keen
dread of ridicule, and the consideration that he
could keep a mistress under closer surveillance
than he could a wife. He knew that he was
ugly and elderly, and that the girl he idolized
could but be to him as a slave. He could not
hug himself with the hope that he might some
day win her heart. He was a cynic by long years
of contempt for his fellow-men—by the habit of
a life unsoftened by friendship or affection, by the
love of kindred or compassion for the poor. He

tried to rest content in his cynicism now; and he told himself that he was as well off as the mighty Shah Jehan, or any other Mohammedan potentate.

He selected the Rue St. Guillaume as a neighbourhood remote from the gay and popular Paris of the Boulevards and the Rue de Rivoli, in which the casual English or American visitor delights; far also from the Champs Elysées and the Parc Monceaux, with their residential population of fashionable artists, and Bohemians of all kinds. The Rue St. Guillaume was old-fashioned, sober, and eminently respectable. He chose a suite of apartments in a grave old house, with an inner quadrangle—a house so grave and silent that the stone quadrangle might have been a cloister. He furnished the rooms with a sombre luxuriousness, and he offered the cage to his snared bird with an air of devoted submission which might have beguiled her into forgetfulness of the bars which shut her in from all the outer world. Upon Madame Quijada he imposed the duty of keeping guard over his sultana. The girl's lightest whim was to be studied and in-

dulged, so long as that whim did not lead to the
gay outer world and its frivolous associations.
Dolores was to be a queen; but her kingdom
was to be within stone walls. She was only to
take air and exercise under conditions of supreme
prudence. She was never to flaunt her beauty in
the Bois de Boulogne at the fashionable hour of
the day; but Madame Quijada had a carriage at
her disposal, in which mother and daughter might
drive in the less frequented suburbs of Paris, or
in the Bois, at an hour when all Paris was else-
where. These restrictions were hard upon a girl
of eighteen, newly emancipated from the monotonous rules and regulations of a convent-school,
and panting for liberty.

"El Santo Corazon was a prison," she complained, "but at least I had fellow-prisoners of
my own age. This is solitary confinement."

She chafed bitterly against the dreariness of
her life, and she detested the man who had made
himself her master; but her mother's stronger
character had acquired complete dominion over
her, and she had neither strength of will nor

courage to rebel against her chains. She submitted to her fate. She wore the jewels which
were her badge of slavery; she gratified her
girlish fancy in surrounding herself with the
loveliest flowers that the South sent to Paris;
and she might, perhaps, have grown reconciled to
her position, and with but the slightest persuasion
might have induced Pedro Perez to give her the
name and status of wife, if she had not been so
unhappy as to fall in love with her cousin, Leon
Duverdier.

During the first year of her residence in Paris,
Duverdier was a frequent visitor in his aunt's
salon. He was about forty years of age, handsome, audacious, plausible, more seductive in his
riper years than a younger lover would have been,
because more experienced in the artifices that
fascinate a romantic girl. He had newly returned
from Spanish America, where he had been living
a roving and adventurous life, now in one state,
now in another, making money no one knew
exactly how, but a familiar figure at the gaming-
tables of every city in which he had his abode.

He came to Paris, set up his laboratory, and described himself as an experimentalist and inventor, on the high road to great and useful discoveries. Perez knew of the relationship between Duverdier and the Quijadas, and had met Duverdier on the Bourse; but he did not know that this handsome cousin was a frequent visitor in the Rue St. Guillaume, since the younger man's visits were always so timed as to avoid the Master of the Prison-house. Had it been otherwise, the old man's jealousy would have been quick to take alarm.

In her utter ignorance of life, Dolores turned to her cousin as the representative of all that is most fascinating and most interesting in the outer world. His flashy and superficial cleverness passed as the versatility of a born genius; she believed all that he told her of his scientific day-dreams, and accepted his inchoate experiments as the first stages in the career of greatness. He was just young enough and just handsome enough to win the heart of a girl who had no opportunity of comparing him with more distinguished men.

It was the policy of his life to make love to every
pretty woman who would listen to him, and he
had even condescended to fascinate ugly women
who were likely to be of use to him. He had
gone through life, from his eighteenth year
upwards, basking in the smiles of beauty, and
relying upon the favour of the gentler sex to
carry him safely over the obstacles in the adventurer's road through life.   Was it likely, then,
that he would neglect his opportunities with
Dolores, a lovely and inexperienced girl who had
the command of one of the deepest purses in
Paris?

He had too holy a fear of his aunt to approach
his cousin in the guise of the seducer; but he
contrived to win her affections, as if unawares,
and she was perhaps all the more blindly in love
with him because he had never asked her for her
heart. He always affected to respect her relations with Perez, and he told her bluntly that
her mission in life was to make the financier her
husband.

"It is your own fault that the marriage has

not come off ages ago," he said; and then, when
the girl answered him only with a deep sigh, it
was his task to console her, his task to talk of the
happiness which might have been had his lot in
life been different.

"I am little better than a pauper," he told her,
"and my life is full of bitter memories. No
woman who values her own happiness should link
her lot with mine."

Dolores pondered over that phrase, "bitter
memories," and she intrepreted it after her own
fancy, which told her that Leon's youth had been
blighted by some dark love story, a tale of fatal
passion and broken hearts, such as she was reading about daily in the novels which were her chief
recreation.

There were times when he talked, in dark hints
and unfinished sentences, of his past experiences
—the women who had loved him and broken
their hearts for him; the one woman, beautiful,
high-placed, a star of loftiest magnitude, whom
he had loved, and in vain.

The girl listened and believed, weak as water,

loving him all the more because her love was unreturned. He was full of tenderness for her by fits and starts; but he gave her to understand that he could never again love as he had loved that great lady who had flung away name, country, home, and reputation for his sake, and who had died a tragical death in the morning of their love.

Duverdier's visits to the Rue St. Guillaume had not been altogether disinterested. He had gone there in times of financial difficulty, and he had extorted more than one so-called loan from Madame Quijada, and had obtained several smaller sums of money, freely and gladly given, from Dolores, who had never been entrusted with the command of large means, and who dared not part with a single jewel from among Perez Peru's splendid gifts, as he had a troublesome way of passing her diamonds in review every now and then.

He would write to her in the course of the day to tell her that he was going to dine with her in the evening, and that he would like to see her in black velvet and diamonds; and Dolores shrewdly suspected that this was only his manner of assuring himself that she had made away with none of his gifts. These magnificent gems had often passed under Duverdier's hands. He had sat in eager contemplation of their pure white brightness as they lay in their open cases on the table before him.

"They are worth a fortune, Dolores," he said, "but they are of very little use to you—of less use than toys to a child. The child can amuse itself with the toys, but you can do nothing with the diamonds. It is not worth the trouble of wearing them when there is nobody to admire you."

"Oh, but they are very pretty," the girl answered childishly, "and I like to have them. Perez told me that there are only about half a dozen women in Paris who have such diamonds, and they are all great ladies."

"Perez told you a lie," her cousin answered harshly. "What of the rich Americans, the men whose money has been made in pork or petroleum, and who give their wives diamonds of six times the value of yours?   Perez is an impostor."

He shut the case with a sharp snap.   Those diamonds always made him angry.   The thought of all that money locked up in velvet and morocco, or shining upon the neck and arms of a girl, aggravated him to madness.   He was always in want of money.   He had had a run of luck on occasions, and had rioted for a brief space in the possession of wealth—but it was the wealth of to-day, not of to-morrow, and the next turn of luck had left him penniless.

He looked at those diamonds on his cousin's neck with hungering eyes, and the thought of them haunted him in his dreams.   The image of that waxen neck haunted him too; and he saw it sometimes with one cruel hand upon it, holding it as in an iron vice, while another hand tore off that dazzling necklace.

Once in a distempered dream he saw the same fair neck streaming with blood.   He hurried to the Rue St. Guillaume early next morning, almost expecting to hear of a calamity; but nothing evi had happened. Dolores met him with a smile, surprised at his early visit.

"I had a horrid dream about you," he said, and she saw that he was ghastly pale. "Where do you keep your jewels?" he asked later, when they had been talking of indifferent subjects.

"Oh, that is mother's business. She has all sorts of contrivances for taking care of them."

"I'm afraid, in spite of all her contrivances, you'll be robbed some day," Leon answered moodily.

Yes, she would be robbed, he told himself. Some vulgar thief would get to know of the wealth that was stowed away in those dull old rooms— wealth in its most concentrated and portable form —and he, her cousin, who had such need of a share in the old financier's spoil, would be told that those jewels had vanished as swiftly and silently as if some wicked fairy had changed them into withered leaves.

Madame Quijada did all she could to discourage her nephew's visits, but some reason, known only to herself, restrained her from actually shutting

her door against him ; and Dolores always welcomed him gladly, appear how and when he
might.   If he was moody, she sympathized with
him, pitying griefs he did not take the trouble to
explain.   If he was rude, she bore with his rude-
ness.   For her he was just that one man upon
earth who could do no wrong.   Fate and Fortune
were to blame for using him badly.

It was now nearly four months since she had
seen him.   A brief note had told her that he was
leaving Paris ; that he was likely to be a wanderer
upon the earth, and that it might be years before
they met again.   She was in despair at this cruel
farewell ; and sent her mother to his lodgings to
find out what had become of him.   On her first
visit Madame Quijada heard only the same statement that had been made to the officer of police,
but on going a month later she found the nest
despoiled.   The law had made a clearance of all
Duverdier's effects, at the suit of his chief
creditor.   The apartment was to be let, and
nobody knew or cared what had become of its
late tenant.

The change in Dolores after her cousin's disappearance was too obvious to escape the keen
eye of Perez. He had always known that she
did not care for him; that she submitted to her
slavery as a fate which she was too weak to resist;
that she loved ease and luxury, jewels and flowers
too well to run away from her gilded nest into
that bleak world of the hewers of wood and
drawers of water, that hard world which to her
ignorance must have seemed as terrible as the
wilderness to the dwellers in cities. He knew
that he held her by the most sordid of ties—the
love of wealth and the fear of penury. He had
seen her listless, weary, indifferent; but he had
never until lately seen her absolutely unhappy;
and jealous doubts were soon aroused by that
inexplicable change. He suspected an intrigue
of some kind, and set a private detective to watch
the house in the Rue St. Guillaume; but the man
discovered nothing. No suspicious person was
seen to approach the house, nor did Mademoiselle
Quijada ever go out alone. He questioned her
closely. He told her that he was sure she had

some secret grief, and he urged her to confide in
him. She protested that there was nothing the
matter. She was tired of Paris. That was all.
Her life was monotonous enough to make any
one unhappy. He had no need to look further
for the cause of her low spirits.

"I am going to Madrid next week. Will you go
with me?" asked Perez.

"Yes, yes. I shall be delighted."

Her face lighted up with pleasure. She gave
her master one of those rare smiles which repaid
him for the richest gift he could offer her.

She was thinking that Leon had most likely
gone to Madrid, and that she would find him
there. She thought she could not be in the
same city with him, and yet not contrive to bring
him to her side. She would make her mother
hunt him out for her, even if she herself were
allowed only to change one prison for another.

Her whole manner altered. She became gay
and talkative, and discussed the journey. How
soon would they start? She was dying to go.

"You want to see your old schoolmates, I

suppose," said Perez, "to make them envious of
your jewels and your beauty?"

"Yes, yes, I want to see them all again," she
answered carelessly.

"But I cannot have you gadding about Madrid
any more than about Paris," said Perez. "The
Spanish capital is almost as wicked as the
French."

"Mother can go and find my old companions.
They may come to see me, I suppose?"

"Surely, Dolores, you would not receive any of
your convent comrades in your position?" said
her mother severely. "Do you forget that to
those girls—honoured and happy wives, perhaps,
now—you would seem an outcast. They would
have nothing to say to you."

Perez looked embarrassed. It was the first
direct attack that Madame Quijada had ever
made upon him in the guise of an injured parent.
The bargain he had made with her had been
arranged upon purely commercial principles—
honour so much—maternal affection so much—
beauty so much. Even the injured feelings of

the defunct Quijada, who might in some distant
planet be aware of what was happening here, had
been considered.   The sum total had been large;
and Perez was therefore unprepared for an out-
burst of wounded honour.

Dolores shrugged her shoulders, and gave an
impatient sigh. She was not endowed with fine
feelings, and cared very little whether the link
that bound her to a master she hated was or was
not sanctioned by Holy Church. The good
opinion of the world would not compensate for an
alliance with age and ugliness.

" Your diamonds must go to my office while we
are away," said Perez, after an embarrassed pause.
"I have burglar-proof safes there which will
accommodate all your jewel-cases. I will take
them away with me to-morrow, and lock them up
with my own hand."

"And what am I to wear while I am in
Spain ? "

" Ah, I forgot. You want to astonish your old
friends. Well, keep the sapphires I gave you a
little time ago, and a few of your smaller trinkets.

The diamonds must be made secure before we start. It would be dangerous to travel with jewels of such value."

" Duchesses carry their diamonds everywhere," said Dolores.

" And duchesses are often robbed—sometimes by their husbands, sometimes by their servants, and occasionally by professional thieves. You had better take my advice in this matter."

Dolores submitted with an air of indifference, and Perez departed, promising to fetch the jewel-cases on the following day.

He came and was told that Dolores was too ill to see him. She had changed her mind. She did not care about going to Madrid. The possibility of meeting people who had known her in her innocent girlhood was hateful to her. This was the gist of what Madame Quijada told him, with much circumlocution, and with some tears wrung from a mother's wounded heart.

Seeing that he listened to her reproaches with patience, and that there was an expression of real distress in his withered old face, Madame Quijada

pursued the subject still further. He was breaking her daughter's heart, she told him. He had
but to open his eyes and he would see that she
was drooping and dying by inches in that dismal
prison-house. The sense of a false position, to
a girl brought up in the convent of El Santo
Corazon, was unendurable. Diamonds were as
dross, material comforts were of no account. The
blighted breath of dishonour had passed over
the fair young life, and it was slowly withering
away.

Perez heard and pondered. He idolized
Dolores, and there was positively no obstacle to
his marrying her, except his keen dread of ridicule, the idea of being laughed at by all Paris as
the wealthy dotard with a girl-wife—the fear that
if she were once his wife she would insist upon
flaunting her beauty in the full glare of the
wickedest city in the world, or that city which
seemed so to him.

"If I were to marry her she would lead me a
wretched life," he said, after some meditative
pacings about the spacious salon; "she would

take advantage of her secure position; she would plunge into the vortex of frivolous pleasures; she would drag my name in the mud, perhaps."

"You have known her long enough to know how simple her ideas are, how easily she is contented."

"That is all very well now that she is under restraint. How can I tell what she would be if she had the authority of a wife?"

"Keep her as a slave then, and let her fade and die. Do not reproach me when the end comes."

There was much more to the same purpose— and the result was total surrender upon the part of Pedro Perez. He would marry Dolores at the Mairie as soon as the law allowed. All he stipulated was that she should continue to lead a life remote from the crowds and amusements of fashionable Paris.

CHAPTER IV.

A GLOOMY RETROSPECT.

PEDRO PEREZ and his beautiful wife started for Madrid upon the evening after their marriage. They travelled with all the comfort that wealth can give. Dolores had her mother and her maid as duenna and attendant. They went to the best hotel in Madrid, where, at the instigation of his wife and mother-in-law, Perez engaged the handsomest suite of rooms upon the first floor.

His dread of ridicule, his jealous doubts and suspicions, prompted him to hide the treasure that he had won for himself; but some natural pride intervened, and he could not refrain from showing himself in the fashionable drives and promenades, with his lovely young wife by his side. Gradually it became known to all the

financial world of Madrid that the beautiful girl
who went about with Pedro Perez was actually
his wife, and visits of ceremony and congratu-
lation became frequent in the amber satin salon
au premier.

Madame Perez accepted the situation with
perfect equanimity, and showed to better advantage as a wife than as a beautiful bird in a gilded
cage. If she was not entirely happy she was at
least better contented with herself and her life
than she had been in the Rue St. Guillaume. So
far from repenting his marriage, Perez grew daily
more devoted to his wife and more anxious to
gratify her. He submitted to all Madame
Quijada's exactions, and allowed himself to be led
by the nose by his mother-in-law as well as by
his wife, and in this placable disposition he returned to Paris, where he at once occupied
himself with the task of selecting a home
that should be worthy of a millionaire's young
and lovely wife.

Everybody whom he knew in Paris had heard
of his marriage, and he had to submit to the

congratulations of his acquaintances, which, as he
was particularly shy, were agony to him. He
also had to endure a good many sly thrusts in
the papers, and more than one caricature of *La
Belle et la Bête;* but he bore it all, and after a
week or two consented to mount an elegant
Victoria with a pair of matchless blacks, and to
show himself in the Bois at the fashionable hour.
A coupé was being built for Dolores, and a
second pair of blacks was being looked for,
Madame Quijada and her daughter being of
opinion that a stud to be distingué must be of
one colour.

After looking at a good many houses, Perez
finally decided upon one in the somewhat
solitary Avenue Reiffschossen, which had been
built for a famous actress during the palmy days
of the Empire—the avenue being then known
as the Avenue Hortense—and which was at least
a mile from the Arc du Triomphe. The house
stood at some distance from the road, and was
concealed by a screen of acacias and other
ornamental trees and shrubs. The garden had

been carefully laid out, and the stables had been
the particular care of the first proprietor, who
was a connoisseur in equine arrangements. This
Italian villa, with its grounds and dependencies,
had cost a fortune, but it was offered to Pedro
Perez for about a fourth part of the original cost.
He liked the property, in the first place because
it was a bargain, and in the second place because
its solitary position gratified his idea of retirement with the wife of his choice. He did not
want to live in the heart of Paris, where Dolores
might be encouraged to set up a salon, and
where the men he knew might find it too con-
venient to visit his handsome wife. That solitary
Italian villa, with its screen of foliage, incon-
veniently remote from the busy haunts of men,
was the very home he desired.

Dolores and her mother both admired the
house, and both complained of its surroundings.
The neighbourhood was a desert. It was on the
wrong side of the Bois for fashion and beauty.
Like all bargains, the property was hardly worth
having.

For once in a way Perez was firm in opposition to his wife's wish. He would buy that house and no other.

"If you would rather go on living in the Rue St. Guillaume," he said, "I won't interfere."

"I detest the Rue St. Guillaume," replied Dolores petulantly; so the Italian villa in the Avenue de Reiffschossen was bought, and Dolores was allowed to furnish the new house after her own fancy, and without any consideration of cost. Only in one matter did her husband exercise his authority, and that was in the choice of the household. All the servants were engaged by him at an office in Paris; but he allowed Louise Marcet to assist him in his choice, and to be present during the negotiations. She was to be housekeeper in the new villa, having shown a talent for management and economy in the Rue St. Guillaume. Madame Quijada was allowed to choose her own suite of apartments on the ground floor, in a wing beyond the principal rooms, which were vestibule, salon, dining, and billiard-room. Dolores had her boudoir, bedroom,

dressing, and bath-room on the first floor, while
her husband had a corresponding set of rooms in
the opposite wing. There were two small rooms
at the back of the house, on the same floor,
divided only by a narrow passage from the suite
occupied by Dolores, and these were appropriated
to Mademoiselle Marcet, as sitting-room and bedroom. A servants' staircase at the end of the
passage brought her in easy communication with
the offices below, and enabled her to exercise a
useful surveillance upon the household. The
servants' bedrooms were on an upper story,
almost hidden by the classic ornamentation of
the roof.

An open loggia formed the central feature of
the façade, and divided the apartments of the
master and mistress of the house, offering a
means of communication in summer time, and
a neutral ground where husband and wife might
meet in their idle hours. Dolores was full of
plans for decorating this loggia in an Oriental
style, so soon as spring should revisit the land.
A Parisian winter did not promise much enjoy-

ment from an open loggia, however architectural and Italian.

The installation in the Villa Perez took place very quietly, though both mother and daughter had suggested a ball, or at least an evening party, in honour of *la pendaison de la crémaillère*. Perez reminded them that they knew scarcely half a dozen people in Paris, and asked where their guests were to come from if they were to give a party.

"Madame Perez has only to hold up her finger in order to fill her salon," replied Madame Quijada, with dignity, "or, in other words, you have but to say to one of the best-known Parisians at your club, ' My wife is going to give a party, and I want you to send out two or three hundred cards of invitation on her part,' and the thing is done. We shall give music, supper, and wines that people will talk of for a week; and after that everybody in Paris will want to come to the Villa Perez."

"A very excellent way of squandering money, and courting discomfort," answered Perez, tartly.

"I bought this house for my wife and myself, not for all Paris."

"I foresee that we shall be as dismal here as we were in the Rue St. Guillaume," sighed Madame Quijada, who did not forego a mother-in-law's privilege of saying disagreeable things.

Finding that society was still forbidden fruit, Madame Quijada sank into a slough of sensuous pleasures, and rejoiced in her luxurious surroundings, her daughter's cordon-bleu, and her son-in-law's wine cellar. She began to regard the midday déjeûner and the seven o'clock dinner as the two chief events of the day. She did ample justice to the produce of Burgundy and Bordeaux, nor did she ever forego the dainty goblet of Chartreuse or Curaçoa, which marked the close of the meal—a miniature goblet from which Titania herself might have drunk, only Titania would hardly have refilled the glass so often. In the afternoon Madame Quijada enjoyed her siesta in true Spanish fashion. In the evening she was more alert, and played écarté with her daughter for small stakes, which she generally

won. If Dolores would not play, there was
always the *souffre douleur* Louise, who had the
whole charge of the household on her shoulders,
and who had to please the three people who
constituted the family. Madame Quijada had
given over the entire duty of housekeeping to
her niece, and rarely rose from her easy-chair
except to be driven in her daughter's Victoria,
or to go to a theatre in the luxurious coupé, when
Perez was disinclined to escort his wife.

Nothing had been heard of Leon since his
disappearance, and his aunt's most earnest desire
was that she should never see his face or hear his
name again. There were episodes in her life
which she wanted to forget, now that she had
attained to that respectability with which wealth
can cover the most doubtful antecedents, as with
a royal mantle. It was in search of oblivion that
she filled and refilled the little Venetian goblet
after déjeûner, or dinner; and there were times
when she felt that all the Chartreuse the good
monks ever distilled would hardly be strong
enough to drown certain haunting memories.

Perez Peru noted his worthy mother-in-law's indulgence in the pleasures of the table, and remarked upon this weakness to his wife.

"If you don't look after your mother, she'll take to drinking," he said one evening, as they drove to a boulevard theatre, leaving Madame Quijada sitting opposite Louise at the little card-table, with flushed cheek and glittering eye.

"Bah, if she has just *une pointe* now and then it can't matter," replied Dolores, carelessly. "Her dinner is the only thing that amuses her. You won't let us give parties, or know any amusing people. You have banished even the poor old Duturques. They were dull, but they were alive, and they were better company than chairs and tables."

"You are very ungrateful, Dolores," Perez answered, with a piteous look. "I have refused you nothing, except to change my manner of life. I have always loved solitude, and hated strange faces. I should not be a millionaire if I had not possessed the power of self-concentration, of living on my own thoughts."

"But now you are a millionaire—and three times a millionaire—you ought to enjoy life."

"To enjoy life is to live quietly with you—to have you all to myself, not to see you surrounded with young people, who would despise your old husband, and teach you to despise him. You talk about giving balls, Dolores. Can you not conceive what torture it would be to me to see you dancing with young men—handsome, fascinating, unprincipled, relentless in their pursuit of the women they admire? Men who would talk of you at their clubs, compare you with the vilest of your sex, discuss your every charm, lay wagers about you—as to who should be your favoured lover, and how soon you could be persuaded to dishonour your husband. I could not endure to see you admired, knowing what admiration means among the young libertines I meet on the Bourse, men who seek to make money only that they may squander it upon women a little viler than themselves. You cannot understand what an old man's love is, Dolores—how jealous, how exacting. You forget

how poor a recompense age ever gets for its
devotion to youth."

"I don't mean to be ungrateful," Dolores
answered, with a deep sigh; and then she turned
her head away from her husband, and studied
the passing carriages, the *flâneurs* upon the broad
asphalte pavement, the glitter and splendour of
the shop windows, shops that seemed designed
only for the accommodation of millionaires.

She was going to the theatre in all her glory
of jewels—diamond stars in her hair, a necklace of
single stones, each gem worth a *rosière's* dower,
diamond serpents in single, double, and treble
coils winding up her slim round arm. She wore
a simple evening toilette of some black gauzy
material, but the Chantilly lace upon her gown
was only second in value to the gems on her
neck. When a beautiful young woman marries
age and ugliness she can at least assert the claims
of beauty by spending her husband's money
royally.

The theatre was the Ambigu, where a new
comedy of Sardou's had just made a hit, and

where all Paris was crowding nightly. Dolores
was indignant when she found that the box her
husband had secured for her was only a small
one on the pit tier, where neither her beauty nor
her diamonds could be adequately seen. He had
his old fancy for these shadowy little boxes, where
it pleased him to hide his enchantress from the
vulgar eye; but in spite of these jealous pre-
cautions, Madame Perez was already known and
talked about as *la belle aux diamants.*

Her husband's reputation as a triple millionaire
gave a special interest to her jewels. People
gloated upon gems which might have cost half
a million, if Perez pleased. He could have
spent half a million, reduced his fortune by a
sixth, without feeling any poorer. "He could
make as much in a week if he chose to start a
new mine," said the *flâneurs* on the Bourse.
"He has but to write a prospectus, and the
money pours in like water. He has a Golconda
in his ink-pot."

While Perez and his wife were laughing at

Sardou's biting wit, Madame Quijada was winning Louise Marcet's half-francs by her astute and studied play. Louise took no interest in the game—indeed hated all games of cards—and only played as a part of her duty in that house where she was the shadow of everybody else's sunshine.

They had played nearly an hour and a half when the elder woman threw down the cards with an impatient sigh, instead of dealing them.

"We have played long enough for to-night, Louise; I am tired of winning such miserable stakes. How ghastly the silence of this house is! Nothing but the tick, tick, tick of that clock on the mantelpiece, and the crackling of the logs now and then. You may get me a finger of fine champagne. I feel very low to-night. This house is killing me."

"You ought to be much easier in your mind now that your daughter has been placed in an honourable position—now that your conscience is at peace upon her account," said Louise, gravely.

"My conscience! Don't preach to me about conscience. I have done with all superstitious bugbears. I finished with them before I left Marseilles. I have never entered a church since my marriage. I was overdosed with religion in my girlhood. I married a clever man, who soon taught me to laugh at the old fables."

"And were you happier, do you think, for abandoning the old pathways?" asked Louise, gravely, arranging the cards, with her eyelids cast down, as if she hardly liked to meet her aunt's eyes while she spoke of sacred things.

"Happier! Happy — happier — happiest! Those are idle words, child. I don't believe anybody is happy. I don't believe in the existence of happiness."

"Oh, you are wrong, aunt! There are moments, hours, days in this life perfectly and beautifully happy—days to which one looks back afterwards as to a dream of Heaven—days to which one looks forward after death, hoping that God will give us back that lost happiness in Heaven. Those brief days are balanced by long

years of misery; but they have been—they have
been. There is nobody on this earth who has
not once been happy. The word is not an idle
invention."

"Well, I suppose I was happy in my time—
happy that Easter night when Jules Delmont
followed me home from the church door, and
talked to me, while my mother walked on ahead
with my elder sister, your mother, little suspect-
ing that I had an admirer making love to me
under cover of the darkness. He was only clerk
to an *avoué*, but those who knew anything about
him said that he was one of the cleverest young
men in Marseilles, and as my parents were only
small shopkeepers they did not make many
objections to my marrying him. We had only a
couple of rooms to live in, and thirty francs a
week to live upon; but it was all bright enough
for the first year; and then—and then I found
out things about my clever young husband.
There was more money, but it wasn't come by
very honestly; and we had to leave Marseilles
one night in secret, never to go back there. We

came to Paris, of course—everybody comes to
Paris—and Dolores was born in a little street
near St. Germain l'Auxerrois, where we struggled
on somehow—till the end came for my husband.
the bitter, cruel end. Are you ever going to get
me that mouthful of cognac ? "

" Yes, yes, aunt, but indeed you would be
better without it."

" How dare you dictate to me! I am sick
and faint with thinking of my wretched past.
Get me some cognac this instant ! "

Louise left the room and returned with a tiny
carafe, and Titania's Venetian goblet. She did
all she could to discourage her aunt's growing
propensity for alcohol, but she was only a
dependent. She might remonstrate, but she was
compelled to obey.

" He was arrested at a low dancing place,
among men and women of the vilest character—
men who were like bad women, women who were
like vicious men," pursued Madame Quijada,
helping herself to the cognac with a tremulous
hand.

" Why dwell upon those bygone troubles ? I know all the sad story."

" It does me good to talk ; anything is better than the silence of this ghastly room—white and gold—so white, so cold and cheerless, like a room meant for ghosts. It is a relief to talk of what I suffered in those days. He was arrested for swindling, forgery, a long series of frauds, and he was taken to prison. I never saw him alive again. He hanged himself at daybreak, within two hours of his arrest—hanged himself with a silk handkerchief upon the iron bar of the prison- grating, before he had been even examined by the *juge d'instruction*, and before his jailers thought it necessary to take any special pre- cautions against suicide."

"You were much to be pitied, aunt," said Louise, quietly, putting away the neat little boxes of cards.

She had heard the story of her aunt's marriage very often of late, for Madame Quijada had grown more loquacious in proportion as she indulged in alcohol. She did not talk of these things to Dolores, who had been brought up in ignorance of her father's character, had, indeed, been brought up to believe that the departed parent was the scion of a noble Andalusian family, whereas the lawyer's clerk of Marseilles was the son of a pettifogging lawyer, and the name Quijada had been only adopted by Dolores' mother when she went to Madrid. She found the name in a volume of Cervantes which she opened at random.

"Oh, I have had a dreadful life, Louise. I have been surrounded by criminals," cried Madame Quijada, after two or three little glasses.

"Don't talk of it, aunt," repeated her niece, with a sudden vehemence. "You ought to be wiser than to talk to me of the past, knowing how much I have suffered—knowing that I shall never cease to suffer from that bitter memory, that the very presence of that man in the room stifles me. I cannot breathe when he is near me. I feel as if I must fall upon him and kill him, as he killed——"

"Hush, hush!" cried her aunt, looking apprehensively towards the door. "You are right. We ought never to talk of the past. It is dangerous, dangerous in every way. Heaven be praised, we have not heard of your brother for six months. We may never hear of him again."

"Ah, I always dread him most, after an interval of absence. He will reappear as he has reappeared before—or, if not, we shall read of some crime that has been committed in some foreign city, and we shall know that it is his work. He has neither heart nor conscience. Can I ever forget, do you think, how he killed the man I idolized—the best and most generous of men? Can I ever forget how he used my name —name for evermore hateful to me—as a lure to draw that good, brave man to his death? And yet he dares to come into a room where I am— he dares to offer me his hand, red with the stain of murder."

"You have no right to fix that crime upon your brother!" Madame Quijada exclaimed angrily. "There is nothing to identify him with the murder, absolutely nothing. Your name

might be used by any one. The unfortunate man
may have talked about you, boasted of his con-
quest in the presence of his servants—of some
French or Italian butler perhaps, who, being in
the house, would know all his master's intended
movements, and all about the money which was
to change hands that day. Servants are often
agents—conscious or unconscious—in crimes that
mystify everybody. You have no right to
associate your brother with that crime."

"I have the right of my own conviction. I
know as well that it was his hand that struck
the blow as if I had been standing by when
the murder was done. I have no doubt about the
murderer. What I want to find out is the
identity of the murderer's accomplice—before
God and man as guilty as the murderer himself.
Who was the middle-aged woman who met
Robert Hatrell in the street, and asked him to
go to Antoinette Morel's deathbed? Who was
the woman who used that lure? Who was the
elderly Frenchwoman who changed the English
bank-notes on the Riviera? Can you answer me

those questions, aunt, you whose bread I have eaten—the bitter bread of dependence—and whose slave I have been, ever since my illness left me unable to grapple with the outside world? I have been afraid to live anywhere else—afraid to be among other people, lest in some moment of dark thought I should betray my brother. He is of my own blood, and I have sworn to myself never to give him up to justice."

"Give him up!" cried her aunt, contemptuously. "Why you have not one shred of proof against him. There is nothing but your own brain-sick fancies to connect your brother with that Englishman's death. You are *toquée*, child, about Robert Hatrell. Your poor brain has never got over the fever that your sick fancies brought upon you; and one ought to be patient with you, and let you talk any nonsense you like. Luckily for your brother the police are not influenced by hysterical women. They want facts, hard facts; and there is not one fact to connect your brother, Claude Leon Morel, with the crime in Denmark Street."

"Or you with the mysterious accomplice," said Louise. "Perhaps not. Yet if you were unconcerned in that foul crime, why did you both change your names within a month of the murder? Why was I made to change my name from Morel to Marcet, and to assume my second baptismal name in place of my first?"

"Your brother had made himself notorious during the Commune. He was not included in the amnesty; and he could not return to France in his own name. He was supposed to have been shot with the others at Satory. His resurrection would have been dangerous."

"Say that the false name meant nothing; but how do you account for the sudden change from poverty to wealth? You and I were living in an attic in a wretched dirty street in one of the shabbiest, dreariest quarters of that great wilderness of brick where we had taken refuge after the troubles here. One day, you disappeared without telling me where you were going, leaving me just a line to say you were going away upon business and might be absent for

some time. You left me penniless, except for
the pittance I was able to earn by working for
a Jewish tailoring house—cruel work, which wore
my fingers to the bone. You had been gone a
week when I heard some women in the court
where I lived talking of a murder. I could just
understand enough English then to know what
they were talking about, but I listened heed-
lessly enough until I heard the name of Hatrell
—not pronounced as I pronounced it, yet a great
horror came over me at the thought that it
might be the same name. It was not he who
was murdered, I told myself; I was an idiot to
be so disturbed by fear. And yet I could not
command myself or keep calm while I questioned
the women. They couldn't tell me who the
murdered man was—only that his name was
Hatrell. They said if I wanted to know more
I had better buy a newspaper. I rushed out
into the street like a mad woman, and it seemed
to me as if I should never find a shop where
they sold newspapers, though there were hundreds
of shops in the long busy street. At last I found

a tobacconist's where there were a lot of papers stuck in a rack against the doorway. I took three of them, haphazard, and gave the shop-keeper the last threepence I had in the world—the pence that were to have bought food for the day. I hurried back to my garret as fast as my feet would carry me. I thought more than once that I should fall down in the street, for my knees seemed to give way under me. I would not trust myself to look at the papers till I was safe in my own hole, like a wounded animal; and then I bolted my door and sat down upon the bare boards and unfolded one of the newspapers."

"Why go over all this old ground, Louise? A little while ago you reproached me for dwelling on the past; and now you are harping upon old sores. You have told me the story often enough."

Louise had begun to pace the room in an agitated manner as she talked, while Madame Quijada sank deeper into her luxurious arm-chair, and sat there looking up at her niece with an awe-stricken countenance, as if she had been

Nemesis. Time was when she would have put down all such speech as this with a high hand; but the growing habit of brandy and chloral had weakened her energies. She who once held so firm a mastery over daughter and niece was now powerless to control either.

"I will talk of these things. You have kept me long enough in miserable silence and submission. I have been your drudge—not because I feared you, or valued the home you have given me—but because I care nothing for my life, and would as soon be a slave as an empress. But there are times when the memory of the past is too strong for me. I want you to know what I suffered while I was alone in that garret. The room comes back to me in my dreams sometimes with a hideous reality, and I fancy I am sitting there in the hot summer afternoon, stitching, stitching in hopeless monotony, as if I were a human machine. I *must* talk of that hideous past. It is in my mind always; it is a part of me."

She walked to and fro in silence for a few

minutes, and then went on recalling her misery,
step by step.

"The first newspaper that I opened was full
of the Denmark Street murder—and the Denmark Street murder was the murder of Robert
Hatrell. I could read English much better than
I could speak it, and there was not one word of
the witnesses that escaped me. I saw my own
name, and understood that it was the name of
his poor Antoinette which had lured him to the
shambles in which he was to be killed. And
then I knew that the murderer was my brother—
my brother, whose face I had not seen since the
first few weeks after we came to London. I
knew that the pretended watchmaker in Denmark Street was my brother, and that the woman
who asked Robert Hatrell to go to the deathbed
of a girl called Antoinette must be you, and
only you. And I knew that because Robert
Hatrell had once been kind to me, and loved me
a little, perhaps, in spite of the difference in our
stations, because of those few happy days of my
girlhood, he had been trapped and murdered.

It was not till afterwards that I read about the changing of the notes on the Riviera; but, when I did, I knew that the grey-haired Frenchwoman was you. I knew your shifty tricks well enough in the past to know that you would have no difficulty in disguising yourself and aping the manners of a woman of quality. That was months afterwards, when I was able to leave the French Hospital, where I was carried raving mad with brain-fever after starving in my garret for nearly a week, trying to work from daybreak till dark, and spending sleepless nights of agony. But for the refuge that blessed institution afforded me I must have died of hunger in my garret, or been turned out of doors to die in the street. My landlord was a cabdriver, and he had the humanity to put me into his cab, burnt up with fever and delirious as I was, and drive me to the hospital, where he told them my story."

"I sent you money as soon as I had settled at Madrid, where I went in the hope of getting help from an old friend."

" Yes, your letter telling me to go to Madrid and enclosing the money for the journey arrived after I had gone to the hospital. The letter was given me when I recovered my senses, and when I was able to travel I set out for Spain. In Madrid I found you established in very different quarters to our garret in the Minories. Your old friend had been very generous to you. You who had been nearly starving in London were able to make a very good figure in Madrid, able to send your daughter to a convent-school, you who were living on bread and water before Robert Hatrell was murdered. Do you suppose I ever doubted where your money came from? I knew from the beginning that it was the price of blood. You called me mad when I refused to eat or drink with you while your prosperity lasted. You laughed at me because I preferred a crust of bread in my garret to your dainty fare. When your money was gone and you were again reduced to poverty my mind was easier; I could better bear to live with you; and then I grew fond of Dolores—she at least was innocent of all evil—and so I learned to bear the burden of my life."

"You are a fool," muttered Madame Quijada, hastily. "I have heard all this rodomontade of yours so often that I never think it worth my while to argue with you. Just give me your arm to help me to my room, before Dolores and her husband come home from the theatre. These rheumatic knees of mine will hardly carry me upstairs without assistance. You are a fool, Louise. You might be a milliner's drudge, toiling among a lot of other drudges at this day, if it were not for your cousin Dolores and me."

"I might have been lying at the bottom of the Seine long ago, if it were not for Dolores," answered Louise, gloomily. "Her love has been the only bond that held me to life."

CHAPTER V.

I AM engaged to Gilbert Florestan. At last I understand what it is to be an engaged girl; and henceforward I shall be able to sympathize with every engaged girl in this world, of whatever nation, of whatever colour, whether she wears ostrich feathers and diamonds in her head at the Court of St. James's, or dances in a feather-girdle on some unknown islet of the South Seas; whether she spends her allowance on frocks or on beads. Yes, till I am ninety, till I am cold in death, I shall be able to sympathize with every lover and every loved one upon earth : for now I know what love means. I know that it means EVERYTHING.

It means the colour of the sky, and the brightness of the sun; it means the perfume of flowers and the freshness of morning : it means the balmy noontide; and it means the restful coolness of green waving boughs: it means lamplight at eventide in cosy, gracious drawing-rooms: it means blind-man's holiday beside the morning-room fire! It means all these; for all these have double beauty, and charm, and comfort, and sweetness since Gilbert and I were engaged.

WHAT will Cyril think, down at the bottom of this round globe, when he hears that Gilbert and I are to be married on the first day of the new year? What can he think, except that I am the lightest and most trumpery young woman he ever had the misfortune to count among his acquaintance?

Beatrice Reardon has been very nice to me. She says that I have nothing to be ashamed about in the transaction. It is customary. It is, one may say, a rule of the game. When people break off an engagement, even if they have been engaged for years, and have doted on each other all the time, it is the duty of each to get engaged to somebody else without the slightest loss of time. They owe this to their own dignity. A girl who has the slightest self-respect will get engaged within a week after the parting, even if she has to marry a chimney-sweep.

"Of course," said I. "That is what Claire does in the 'Ironmaster,' and every one knows what a perfect heroine she was."

"If you can just tolerate Mr. Florestan, you may consider yourself very lucky," said Beatrice. "When I heard you were going to marry him, I made up my mind that he was absolutely loathsome to you."

"Did you?" cried I. "Curious, isn't it? I really can just submit to the idea of my future existence as his wife. I shall live next door to mother, and that will be some consolation."

I meant to write everything in this diary. It was to be my novel, the romance of my life, with all its bright colours and all its dark shadows. It was to be a book to whose pages I could go back when I am middle-aged and when I am old, and live again all the happiest hours of my youth, and awaken echoes of old voices and vivid smiles, and every thought, feeling, and

fancy of the passing hour. The wheels of the
chariot roll on so swiftly when one is happy.
One should try at least to put a break upon
memory; and for that there is only one way—
pen and ink.

Yes, I meant the story of my life to be
complete; and yet I am going to leave one little
blank. A little blank, did I say?—a blank which
represents the crisis of my existence, the turning
point between dull patience and consummate
bliss.

I cannot write the mood and manner of my
engagement, that sudden passage from liberty to
bondage, when he took me in his arms, in the
arbour where we were once so miserable, and
called me "wife." Wife! As if we were married
already! Absurd, no doubt, to the indifferent
reader, but the word thrilled my heart.

I cannot write of his kisses, or reckon them as
if they were pounds, shillings, and pence in the
housekeeper's book. I cannot write all the sweet
foolishness of his talk, the undeserved praises, the
intoxicating flatteries, which he protested were

not flatteries. Of those ridiculous moments I can keep no record. Perhaps if I had been let in at the gate of Paradise for half an hour I should not be able to describe the heavenly garden when I came out again. It is the same with that half-hour in the arbour. He talked, and I listened, and we were engaged. That is my only record.

On the same evening, however, we had a very serious conversation on the terrace after dinner. Mother was in her favourite seat by the drawing-room window. Uncle Ambrose was pacing the room. We could see them both in the lamplight as we walked slowly up and down. The evening was wonderfully warm and balmy for the end of September, and the great full moon was rising behind Lamford Church tower; this being the third moon we have worn out since we left London.

We talked of the moon a little, and he quoted Shelley, whom he knows as well as if he had competed for one of Mrs. Crawshay's prizes; and then I ventured to ask him a question which had been burning my tongue ever since we were engaged, just four hours and a half. It is wonderful what those four hours had done for me. I felt as much at my ease with him as if we had been engaged for three weeks; and I began to understand the cool audacity of girls who send their fiancés on messages and make light of them in company, and the free and easy manners of the motherly girls who mend their sweethearts' gloves, and scold them for spilling things on their waistcoats, and put diachylon-plaster on their wounds.

"Will you be very angry if I ask you a question?" I asked.

"I should be angry if you wished to ask me anything and didn't," said he. "'Being your slave, what should I do——'"

"Please don't," I cried. "Cyril quoted that sonnet once, and I was quite rude to him about it. I shouldn't like you to quote anything second-hand. Yet it is a lovely sonnet, isn't it?" I added apologetically, for the line sounded sweet from *him*. "Cyril was not in touch with my ideas about Shakespeare."

He laughed, and answered with a most un-
necessary kiss.

"You really wouldn't mind?" I asked.

"From those lips all words are dear."

"Were you ever in love with anybody before
you began to care for me?"

"Ah, I thought that question would come.
Shall I answer it Jesuitically or honestly?"

"Oh, honestly, please; be brutal to me rather
than dishonest. Of course I am prepared for the
worst. You must have adored ever so many
girls before you happened to let your glances
light upon insignificant me."

"Ever so many. That's a large order. Suppose I plead guilty to two. I wish I had never
looked at a woman, or at least never wasted a
thought upon one till I saw you. I shouldn't, if
I had only known what was coming."

"Do you really think I am as nice as the other
two?" I asked, comforted by those sweet words.

"I think you are to them as a wild rose on a
hedge in the dewy morning compared with a
double dahlia in the heat and dust and glare of

a tent at a flower show. You are as the freshness
of the morning, and they smelt of gas. The first
could not help that, poor soul, for it was across
the footlights my heart went out to her."

" Was she very pretty?" I asked.

"She was very pretty. That was just fifteen
years ago, mark you, when I was at Eton. She
is very pretty at this present hour; she will go
on being very pretty, I hope, till the end of the
century. She is a burlesque actress, and I saw
her in the daintiest little villager's dress you can
conceive, dancing as lightly as a real fairy, and
not a stage one. Yes, Daisy," he said gravely,
" I plead guilty to being over head and ears in
love with Miss Millicent Melville, of the Hilarity,
fifteen years ago, for the whole space of the
Christmas holidays. I was stone-broke for her
sake, and spent all my tips upon theatre tickets,
hothouse flowers, and chocolate caramels. I delivered the flowers and the caramels to the surly
stage doorkeeper, who may have sold them to the
minor members of the troupe for aught I know.
I never got speech of my houri; and I was heart-

broken when I discovered, upon unimpeachable
authority, that she had a husband and five
children. How she did it—how she looked so
lovely and sylphlike and childishly innocent,
with an eating and drinking, smoking and swear-
ing man and five brats to work for I have never
been able to understand."

"Was she number one?" I asked.

"Yes, she was number one."

"In that case I forgive you your first love.
And now tell me about your second."

"That is a graver case, Daisy. I cannot make
light of that infatuation. Cupid did not assail me
with paper pellets that time. His arrows were
barbed, and the barbs were poisoned. I loved a
woman who was unworthy of my love, Daisy. I
passed through the scathing fire of a wasted
passion——"

"You loved her as well as you love me?" I
asked, feeling just as if I had dropped from a paradise in yonder moon down to a hard, cruel earth.

All my gladness perished in one gasping sigh.
I felt sure he had cared more for her than for me.

"I'm afraid 1 must plead guilty to having loved her very dearly while my love lasted, Daisy; but the cure was a clean cure. There was not so much as a scar left from the old wound by the time I met you in Paris; and from that hour I was yours and yours only."

"And if I had not broken with Cyril, what would you have done?"

"Dragged on my roaming, desultory life, and suffered the dull agony of an empty heart."

"Were you really unhappy in Scotland, in spite of grouse and salmon?"

"In spite of as a fine a stag as was ever stalked, which this hand slew the day before I casually heard that Arden had sailed in the big new steamer for Colombo."

"And would you not have found some new divinity before Christmas?"

It was delightful to have him there and to be able to catechise him: yet I could not help being savagely jealous of that unknown love, the number two in his calendar.

I could not but feel that it was nice of him to

tell me the truth, even at the risk of offending me for life.

"Tell me about that second flame of yours," I said, agonized with curiosity. "Was she very lovely?"

"She was splendidly handsome—a woman whose diamonds seemed more brilliant than those of other women, because they so harmonized with her bright beauty. I was among many worshippers, and I happened to be the most eligible of her adorers from a matrimonial point of view, and so she was gracious to me, and so I was her slave——"

"Did she jilt you?" I asked, for there was a bitterness in his tone which assured me the dear creature had treated him abominably.

I could have hugged her for it.

"Well, it was hardly a case of jilting. If I were to write my story I should call the book 'Illusion and Disillusion.' I was fortunate enough to find her out—before marriage instead of afterwards. My innocent little Daisy can hardly guess what a world of misery that discovery saved me."

"I don't want to guess," I said; "but there is one thing I should like to know, Gilbert."

I blushed in the moonlight, and trembled at my own audacity as I pronounced his Christian name.

I had my arm through his, and found myself giving his arm a gentle squeeze now and then, just to make sure that he was real, and that all the ecstasy of this hour was not a moonlit dream.

"Ask as many questions as you like, fair Fatima. There is no blue chamber in my memory of which you may not open the door."

"It does not pain you to speak of that wicked person?"

"Not a whit. No more than it would pain me to talk of Cleopatra."

"But at the time of your disillusion—did love die all at once, or by inches?"

"Love died in an hour; but there was something, the memory and after-taste of passion, which was plaguily long a-dying."

"Is it dead yet?" I asked, frightened.

"Dead as a doornail. Dead as Scrooge's

partner, old Marley; deader, for no ghost of that vanished feeling will ever haunt me. I was heart-whole the night I met you at the Grand Opera, and from that night I was your slave."

"Oh, that is nonsense!" cried I; "you could not have cared for me all at once, a commonplace English person like me. What was there in my poor face to catch your eye?"

"Innocence, truth, candour. The virtues which make man's life happy and honourable. I saw poetic loveliness, and through that transparent beauty I saw the true and pure heart of girlhood, a heart of virgin-gold, flawless, above price."

"Don't, don't!" I cried, standing on tiptoe to put my hand upon his lips. "This last illusion is worse than the first and second. How can I ever live up to such an ideal as you have made out of me?"

"Only love me, Daisy; there is no more to do."

"Oh, that comes too easy. I did that before I was asked."

Mother's voice calling us from the open
window put an end to our confidential talk, but
my heart was quite at ease now that I knew the
history of his earlier loves. If he had told me
he had never been in love before he saw me I
should not have believed him; and I should
have been tortured for all the years to come by
inextinguishable distrust.

All this happened nearly a month ago, though
I couldn't bring myself to write about it before
to-day; and perhaps I should not be writing
now if Gilbert had not been obliged to go to
London to see his solicitor—our first parting—
leaving me to get through the day somehow
without him. The grounds look so dreary, the
shrubberies seem so empty—and oh! what ages
to eight o'clock dinner, when he will be back.

CHAPTER VI.

DAISY'S DIARY IN SORROW.

WHEN I wrote the last line in this book, I think
I must have been the happiest girl in the world.
There was hardly a cloud upon my sky—yes, one
cloud, the fact that the man whom I thought
my friend and benefactor was out of health and
unhappy. Yet, in spite of that one cloud I was
utterly happy, selfishly absorbed in my new
happiness.

To-day I take up my pen in fear and
trembling. A dark and terrible cloud has closed
over my life.

I thank God that cloud does not rest upon my
lover's head. He stands out in the sunshine, and
all my thoughts of him are full of thankfulness
and delight; but I can no longer be the selfish,
self-absorbed creature I was when I wrote those

last foolish pages, giving myself up to this dumb
confidant as I could do to no living being. I
must think of others now. This dark discovery
forces my thoughts into other grooves. I must
remember that I am my mother's daughter, as
well as Gilbert's affianced wife.

Oh, it is all so sad, so awful, such a cruel
revelation, changing the whole colour of life,
stripping off the mask from a face that was once
honoured and beloved, opening a deep well of
baseness and iniquity in the flowery garden-
world where I was so happy! To me it was as
startling and sudden and blighting to come face
to face with that great wickedness as it would
have been to Eve in Eden, if the ground had
opened at her feet and showed her a charnel
house, there in that fair world where she had
never heard of death.

Sometimes, for a few moments, I doubt, and
ask myself if I am not deluded; if that hideous
suspicion which grew in an hour into absolute
conviction might not after all be groundless;
and then I go over the facts slowly, in cold

blood, one by one, carefully putting them together again, like the pieces in a puzzle, and there the awful fact appears in unmistakable certainty.

Oh, father, father, how that trusting open nature, that generous heart of yours was cheated! How coldly, deliberately, and heartlessly your life was plotted away by the man who sat at your table, and smiled beside your hearth, and was to you almost as a brother! It was your own familiar friend who planned your murder.

I must go back to the moment when this hideous secret revealed itself. It was natural that as Gilbert's fiancée I should tell him every-thing that had happened to me in all my life; and, indeed, I fear that I must have bored him sadly since we were engaged by prattling to him about every detail of my insignificant existence —my lessons, my boat, my playfellows and friends. I don't believe I have spared him a single doll, certainly not a favourite doll, nor a single nursery anecdote, nor a single family joke. He has been told everything.

Two days ago he came into the drawing-room just as it was growing dusk. He had been to London again, and we had had another parting, and I had felt very mopy all the afternoon, more especially as mother had gone off on her weekly round, to hear her weekly tale of woes and ill-nesses. I did not expect to see Gilbert until dinner-time; and oh, how my foolish heart thrilled with delight when I heard his step in the hall just after the clock struck five!

It is not very often that I have the privilege of making tea for Gilbert, and on this occasion I am sorry to say I made it so strong that it was hardly drinkable. I saw he made a wry face at every sip—though he declared it was quite the nicest tea he had ever tasted—and even chivalry did not enable him to empty his cup.

"Was it Metternich or some other great diplomat who sipped a glass of castor oil with every sign of relish because his host had offered it to him as particularly fine Tokay?" I asked him, laughing at his self-sacrifice; and then I rang and ordered some chocolate à la vanille,

which our butler makes to perfection. "You
poor victim of soft-heartedness," I said, "why
did'nt you tell me that the tea was horrid? I
over-reached myself in my endeavour to make it
especially good, so that you might have a high
opinion of my domestic capabilities."

"I like strong tea," he answered, "but
certainly yours is *fortissimo*. I fancy a good-
sized pot of such stuff would serve to blow up
the Houses of Parliament."

How gay we were, as we sat and talked and
laughed in the growing dusk, with our feet on
the marble curb, crooning over the fire like John
Anderson and his old wife! How proud I felt of
my lover, and how blissful in the assurance that
he was all my own, that I had left no corner of
his heart unexplored, no secret hidden from my
prying eyes!

We sipped our chocolate, which was really
delicious. What superior creatures servants are!
If I had attempted to 'make that Menier à la
vanille I have no doubt the result would have
been "ojous," as dear Mr. Toole says in "The

Upper Crust." We sipped our chocolate, and talked and talked, not from grave to gay, but from gay to grave; and presently I told my dearest the single secret of my life, the one act of mine which I had hidden from the best of mothers.

I told him how, when I first went to London, I was haunted by the ghastly vision of my father's murder, and how a morbid longing to see the room where that dark deed was done took possession of my mind, and would not be driven away.

I told him how I crept out of the house in the summer twilight, and described every step in that dismal pilgrimage till I came to Church Street, on my way home. And then I told him of that intolerable Frenchman's insolence, and of the good creature in the hansom, to whom I should *so* like to leave a legacy when I am old enough to make a will, if I only knew his honourable name.

"I know my enemy's name well enough," said I, "for, as the cab was driving off with me, his friends called out to him, 'Holà, Duverdier.'"

"Duverdier!" cried Gilbert, starting as if he
had been shot. "Great God in Heaven! Why,
that is the name of the man I believe to be your
father's murderer!"

In the next instant he seemed to regret having
spoken, but I would not let him take back his
words. I made him tell me all he knew or
thought or suspected about my father's cruel
death; and stage by stage I got the whole story
out of him. It was slow work, for he was sorely
disinclined to tell me anything.

"Now that I know something I must know
all," I said, when he refused to answer my questions; and so, little by little, I heard the whole
story.

My mother had asked him to help her in
tracing out a girl whom my father admired and
had half a mind to marry before he had ever
seen mother's face. She appealed to Gilbert,
counting on his knowledge of Parisian life, and
he had succeeded beyond his hopes up to a
certain stage; but just as he had put his hand,
as it were, upon the brother of this French-

woman, whom he believed to be the so-called watchmaker in Denmark Street, the man left Paris, leaving no clue to his destination.

"I could do no more than leave the case in the hands of the Parisian police, who have a strong motive for finding your father's murderer, if he is above ground," said Gilbert "Of course my reasons for believing this to be the man are in a measure conjectural, but the circumstantial evidence is strong. The man who murdered your father was a man who knew the story of your father's youthful love affair, and was able to use the French milliner's name as a decoy. It is known that Morel was in London with other Communists at the time of the murder; it is known that he was heard of at Madrid soon after the murder, and that he was then flush of money. For my own satisfaction, I have convincing proof that this Duverdier is the man Claude Morel, but it is not such proof as could be produced in a court of justice. The evidence that convinced me was the evidence of a woman's face."

And then he told me how he had met Morel's

sister, and had taxed her with her identity with the girl whom my father once loved. Her emotion at the sound of my father's name was pitiable; her agitation when he accused her brother of the murder was terrible. After that interview he had no doubt as to the guilt of the man now known as Leon Duverdier.

"The one missing link in the chain of evidence is the means by which the knowledge of your father's movements on that fatal day was transmitted to the murderer. He must have had an informant, if not an accomplice, either in the immediate vicinity of this house, or in the lawyer's office, where the hour and the nature of his appointment may have been known to the clerks."

A deadly chill crept through my veins as he said these words. I was glad of the growing darkness which hid my face from him. I was glad that I had deferred the lighting of the lamps, so as to prolong our blind-man's holiday. I sat silent, motionless, paralyzed by the horrible suspicion which filled my mind.

Some one at Lamford must have given the information that enabled the murderer to plan his crime. Who could that some one be unless it were the familiar friend, the confidant of every enterprise and every idea of my father and mother? My mother has told me in answer to my questions that no servant in the house knew where my father was going or what he was going to do that day. The conversation at dinner on the previous evening had not touched on the business part of the transaction. My father had been full of the landscape-gardener's plans, and the talk had been wholly of the terraces and the arboretum, of levelling and planting, and laying on water for fountains and greenhouses. All that was known in the household on that evening or on the following morning was that my father was going to London, and was to return before dinner. Yet some one had furnished such precise information that my father's murderer was able to meet him midway between the bank and the lawyer's office. Who was that accomplice, or worse than accomplice, of the murderer—since

the idea of murder might never have entered
Claude Morel's mind if some one, knowing my
father's affairs, had not told him how large a sum
of money might be gained by that crime?

Who could that secret assassin, that worse than
murderer, be but the man whose footsteps were
now dogged by the shedder of blood?—who, but
that man whose face bore in every line the marks
of an unextinguishable remorse, the man whom I
had seen shrinking away with horror-stricken
countenance from the room where my father used
to sit, and where his guilty conscience may have
conjured up the shadow of the dead?

His friend, his generous, confiding friend! Oh
God, what a depth of iniquity! To have
deliberately planned that cruel murder, to have
plotted the crime which a vulgar assassin was to
execute, to have waited and watched for the
opportunity, perhaps to have tempted and persuaded the assassin, against some remnant of
better feeling, some instinctive shrinking from
bloodshed, some scruple of conscience! And to
have been with us, day by day, after that devilish

act, our friend, our consoler ; till at last, trading
on a woman's gratitude for fancied benefits, he put
forward his claim to the wife of his victim, and
possessed himself of the object of his wicked love!

Possessed himself! Yes, thank God, I know
that my mother never loved him, that she gave
her life up to him as if in payment of a debt,
sacrificing herself to reward the fidelity of a life-
long friendship.

God keep her from the horror of knowing what
I know !

My long silence made Gilbert uneasy about
me, and he was full of tender sympathy, thinking
that our conversation about my father had re-
newed an old grief. Mother came in while he
was consoling me, and the lamps were brought,
and I had to put on a cheerful countenance somehow for her dear sake ; and by-and-by I had to
sit down to dinner with that Judas, and still to
play the hypocrite. I could hear the sound of
my own voice as I talked, and it had such a false
tone that it jarred upon my ear.

Oh, the horror of that hour in the drawing-
room, when mother asked me to play some of
those quaint old variations she and I are so fond
of, and when I sat before the piano and played
like a machine, while Ambrose Arden walked up
and down, with soft, catlike step, and now and
again paused and stood behind me for a few
minutes, and once even laid his hand upon my
shuddering shoulder. My whole being was one
sense of horror and revulsion. I could scarcely
breathe while he was so near me; yet I went
on playing somehow, always like a machine.
Poor Mozart!

"You are not in your usual form to-night,
Daisy," said Gilbert, who pretends to think a
great deal of my playing.

And then he came over to me, and bent down
to look into my eyes, and talked to me ever so
sweetly, and his dear presence exorcised the
demon, and that guilty wretch walked slowly
away, and went on with his restless prowling, to
and fro, to and fro, like a spirit in hell—the hell
of guilty memories and gnawing thoughts, the hell

of the traitor and murderer, that hell within the soul of man which made Judas hurl back his fatal thirty pieces upon his tempters, and rush out into the field and destroy himself.

Where their worm dieth not and their fire is not quenched.

That is the hell which Ambrose Arden has made for himself.

I went on playing while Gilbert went back to the other end of the room where he had been sitting with mother, and challenged her to a game at chess. I was alone in the shadowy corner by the piano, and as I played I watched that tall, slim figure, with the bent shoulders, moving slowly to and fro, with a gliding motion.

Since this awful truth has revealed itself, I seem to see Ambrose Arden in a new light—as if I had been blindfold before, and had made for myself an image of the man, and coloured it with my own colours. The face and figure I watched to-night are new and strange, and the signs of a guilty conscience, the indications of a crafty and double nature seem to me now so strongly im-

pressed upon every look and movement of the
man that I tell myself I *must* have been blind all
this time, or I could not have missed his secret.
It is there, written upon his brow, the very brand
that seared the forehead of the first murderer,
Cain.

What a relief it was to be alone at last! yes,
even a relief to bid good night to Gilbert and
mother, and to lock the door of my own room,
and to sit down by the fire, face to face with the
grim and hideous truth. I wanted to think out
my horrible idea, to arrange all the facts which
seem to constitute such damning evidence
against my step-father, to try if I could not
acquit him, or, at any rate, write "not proven"
against his crime.

Alas, no! After long hours of thought, after
a long winter night without one interval of
blessed sleep, my reason still condemns him. In
my mother's second husband, in the friend and
teacher of all my early years, the man to whom I
owed so much—in him whom last of all men I

should have suspected, I still see the murderer of my father.

I recalled Duverdier's appearance in Grosvenor Square, his persistence in seeing my step-father, his look of baffled fury as he left the house. I recalled his appearance in this place. Would any man without credentials of a guilty nature dare so to haunt a man in my step-father's position ?

Yet this mere fact of the man's persecution would not influence me to believe in my step-father's guilt. The evidence that is to my mind conclusive is the evidence of Cyril's appearance and Cyril's conduct upon the day when he played the listener to a conversation between his father and Duverdier. I saw those three figures in the lane : Ambrose Arden and Duverdier side by side, Duverdier talking angrily, vehemently, though in a lowered voice, and that other figure following stealthily, listening with bent brow and pallid face.

Was it like my frank and manly Cyril to play the spy upon his father's movements, to creep at his father's heels and listen to a confidential conversation? What could be more unlike his character, as I have known it? Nothing but the most stringent circumstances would have forced him into such a contemptible position.

And within two or three hours of that scene in the lane he came to me, changed and aged as if by a mortal malady, and told me that all was over between us. I remember almost every word of our conversation, his protest that the motive of his renunciation was one which I could never know, his resolution to go to the uttermost end of the earth, to begin a new life, to cut himself adrift from all old associations. And this determination, this abandonment of the whole scheme of his existence, had been resolved upon since he left the Rectory, in high spirits, the most light-hearted of men. What but some awful revelation could so quickly change the whole colour of his life?

This is the evidence that weighs most heavily with me; and next to this is the evidence of my step-father's decay, the gradual deepening of the

gloom that has darkened over him in the midst
of the happiest and fairest surroundings.

No, I have no doubt now as to the brain which
plotted the murder, or the hand which sent the
information to the murderer on the eve, or on the
morning, of the fatal day.

And my mother is this man's wife, and must
never know his guilt, lest the horror of it should
drive her mad. When I think of her abiding
love for my father, and think how she gave herself to this Judas, not caring for him, I am almost
mad myself.

Oh, what a cheat and trickster, what a prince of
villains he has been, to play so patient a part, to
sow the wicked seed at the first chance Fate gave
him, and then to wait seven years for the harvest!
Had he asked my mother to be his wife within a
year or two of the murder, her eyes might have
been opened, she might have suspected that he
had some part in her husband's death. But after
seven years of tranquil, self-abnegating friendship,
after winding himself into our hearts by every
artifice of an accomplished hypocrite, it seemed

almost a natural, inevitable development that he should change from friend to lover, and that his constancy in friendship should claim its reward.

No, the dear mother must never know this hideous secret, if any power of self-repression on my part can keep it from her. And so I have day after day to sit at table with the man who planned my father's death; and I have to repress all signs of repulsion, and to seem all that I once was to him, at least in my mother's presence.

Happily for me he spends the greater part of his existence in the solitude of the cottage over the way; happily for all of us that existence is not likely to be a long one. Our Lamford doctor, who went up to London with mother and her husband to assist at the visit to the physician, told Gilbert in confidence that there is organic disease of the heart, and that Ambrose Arden is not likely to live to old age.

CHAPTER VII.

THE AMIABLE MAGICIAN.

ELDERLY men, when they are in love, are the
weakest of mortals, and weakness is prone to
compromises. In his conduct towards his
beautiful young wife, Pedro Perez showed all
the weakness of an elderly lover. He halted
between two opinions. He wanted to keep his
treasure secluded from the world, secure from
the pursuit of Parisian treasure-seekers, and yet
he wanted to flaunt his happiness before the
eyes of those half-dozen or so of competitors and
rivals with whom he had ridden neck and neck
in the *chasse aux millions*—the great race for
wealth which is the favourite sport of this nine-
teenth century, whether the course over which
it is run be the Stock Exchange or the gaming-
saloon, the silver mine or the manure heap.

For Pedro Perez the world meant one particular group of men at his club, one particular corner at his restaurant, and all his ideas of society were limited to that narrow circle of men who had begun life with a five-franc piece and were ending it with four or five millions sterling. To these few intimates Perez had boasted of his wife's beauty, and of the villa in which he had enshrined his idol, as it were in a temple of silver and gold; and these on more than one occasion had expressed their desire to be admitted within the veil of the temple and to behold the goddess.

Perez coquetted with the situation. He declared that his young wife was of too retiring and modest a nature to endure the gaze of strangers; he compared her to the violet shrinking within the shelter of its leaves; but his friends were not to be put off so easily.

"There never was a woman yet who did not like to be admired," said Joffroy, the famous contractor, who, like Perez, had made his fortune in Spanish America, but in another line of

business; "and if your wife is a clever woman
she will like to make the acquaintance of men
of the world, like Hausroth yonder and myself.
I have heard of your wife when she was only
Mademoiselle Quijada, living in retirement with
her mother. A starveling pianoforte player who
teaches my daughters was loud in his praises
of the young lady. I can understand your not
caring to introduce your friends to her while she
was Mademoiselle Quijada, when you might have
run the risk of losing her; but now that she is
your wife it is a miserly thing to keep your
friends on the outside of your door, and I'll be
bound the lady resents her seclusion."

Perez could not bring himself to deny the
charge. He argued with himself that there
could be no danger in allowing Dolores to
receive old fogies like Joffroy and Hausroth,
than whom Paris could hardly furnish two less
attractive men; the former, oily of complexion
and obese of figure, with greasy iron-grey hair
and a bottle nose; the latter, lean and lantern-
jawed, with foxy hair and beard, and the features

of a modern Shylock. The men who begin life with five francs and die worth five millions sterling have very little leisure to sacrifice to the graces. Life with them means to eat and drink and calculate, to invest and reinvest, to watch the money-market with an unwavering vigilance, and to concentrate all the forces of mind and body upon one great aim.

No, there would be no risk in tantalizing these old comrades of the Bourse with a glimpse of his elegant domicile and his lovely and amiable wife; and in conceding thus much he would conciliate Dolores and her mother. He had refused to give a ball; he might compromise the matter by an occasional dinner-party—a small snug dinner, at which only wealth and mature years should be represented.

"I have not many friends, Dolores," he said to his wife that evening, as she sat yawning on a low ottoman in front of the wood fire, while he smoked his after-dinner cigarette, "but the few I have are devoted to me, and they are dying to know you. I don't care about giving a dance, as I told you the other day. I don't want to see my house turned out of windows to please a crowd of young fools whose only claim to notice is that they can imitate a tee-totum; but I've no objection to giving a dinner now and then, if you like."

Dolores stifled a yawn before she answered. She had been looking at the burning logs in a waking dream, and this suggestion of a dinner-party did not arouse any enthusiasm in her.

"The people you know are so dreadful," she said. "You have pointed out men in the Bois as your dearest friends, whose appearance positively made me shudder. A long lantern-jawed man with red hair, and a threadbare overcoat, for instance."

"Hausroth," murmured Perez, recognizing the picture; "a man only second in importance to the Rothschilds and the Mires."

"And a bloated creature, with a complexion that suggests nothing but the refuse of the oil-mills."

"Joffroy."

"And a little wizened wretch, with one shoulder higher than the other, and long greasy hair of a greenish grey."

"Struoski," said Perez, "a Pole by birth, and the keenest financier in Paris. Do you know, Dolores, the amount of solid capital which those three men represent?"

"I neither know nor care. All I hope is that they will never cross my threshold; unless, indeed, you allow me to get together so many artistic and agreeable people that I shall hardly be conscious of your capitalists."

"Where are you to get your agreeable people?" asked Perez, after a pause of discomfiture, vexed that his compromise found so little favour with his idol.

"Oh, I will find them easily enough, if you only give me leave to send out a few invitations. Duturque knows lots of clever people, and he can send out my cards: 'Monsieur and Madame Perez invite Monsieur or Madame Chose to spend the evening with them'—with 'Monsieur Duturque's compliments' at the corner of the card."

"But have you ever met these people in Madame Duturque's salon—a third floor in the Rue des Saints Pères?" inquired Perez, incredulously.

"Certainly not. They would not go to a floor in the Rue des Saints Pères. They would not go anywhere to be entertained with Duturque's music and Madame Duturque's weak tea; but they will come to my villa; they will come to the wife of Perez Peru. Voyons, mon ami, let us make a compromise——"

Perez sighed. It was his own word.

"You shall invite those dreadful-looking human ingots of yours to dinner, a dinner of all that is most precious in the way of gormandize; and after dinner, I, Madame Perez, will be at home to all that is most distinguished in the art world: the painters and sculptors; the actors and actresses; the journalists——"

"Who will write about your party in their accursed papers, and who will ridicule your husband?"

"Why should they ridicule you? Is it

ridiculous to have married youth and good looks instead of age and ugliness? I can't understand, Pedro, why you are so ashamed of your wife."

She lighted a cigarette for him as she talked, seating herself caressingly upon the arm of his chair, and transferring the cigarette delicately from her lips to his. She knew that he was yielding, and that a caress and a few sweet words would clench the bargain.

" Ashamed of my wife ! no, it is of the contrast between wife and husband I am ashamed. It is that which the newspaper men will ridicule."

" They will be too wise to offend so powerful a man as Perez Peru."

" Ah, but they have lampooned me ; they have seized every occasion to hold me up to ridicule."

"Simply because you live in your shell like a snail. You are of no use to the clever people of Paris. You fulfil none of the duties of a millionaire. You will be a few thousands richer when you die, but you will have offended every-

body while you live. Give me *carte blanche*,
Pedro, and you shall have all the comic
journalists and caricaturists at your feet. There
shall be no dancing, there shall be no foolish
young men; but I will give a party that will
dazzle Paris."

He did not yield without a struggle. He
smoked a third and a fourth cigarette of his
wife's lighting. Her gentleness, her graceful
coquetries made him forget every resolution he
had ever made to live his own life and to keep
the tinsel and folly of the pleasure-loving world
outside his gate. He yielded after the fourth
cigarette, as Ahasuerus might have yielded to
Esther, when Esther was still the latest novelty
in the Royal harem.

"Do what you like, ma chérie. Invite whom
you please," he murmured at last.

The cards of invitation went out two days after
that discussion. The list of names was written
with the aid of the good Duturque, whose professional career had brought him into communication with the art-world of Paris, though

it had not elevated him to intimacy with celebrities. Dolores trusted much to her own reputation as a beauty whose charms had been hidden from the outer world. The cards despatched, she went to the chief confectioners, electricians, florists, and wine-merchants of Paris. She called in upholsterers and tent-makers. She arranged for a series of three large marquees, which were to cover the lawn behind her villa. The house in all its beauty and splendour was to be only a vestibule to these tented halls. The first marquee was to be decorated with palms and tropical plants, and was to serve as a promenade pure and simple. Her drawing-room was to be the entrance to this outer tent, and here she was to receive her guests. The second marquee was to be decorated contrastively with tapestries and Oriental brocades, and here there was to be a concert by some of the first artistes in Paris and in the world. The third and largest tent was the supper-room, a supper served upon small round tables, and which was to last from midnight till two o'clock.

For this tent Dolores had imagined, and the electricians had carried out, the most distinguished feature of the entertainment. From the silken dome in the centre of the immense circular marquee hung a monster egg-shaped lamp, a lamp of opaline hue, shedding the mildest, milkiest, moonlight radiance upon the supper-tables and the supper-eaters.

This was the roc's egg; and Dolores and her dressmaker had arranged a costume which, without being absolutely a fancy dress, should be so far Oriental in character as to suggest the Princess Badroulbadour.

It was very long since Madame Quijada's daughter had seemed so gay and girlish as in the fortnight during which the upholsterers and electricians and tent-makers were preparing for this eccentric entertainment. Her delight had something of childishness in it, no doubt, but that very childishness fascinated Pedro Perez, and he soon found himself taking as keen an interest in the approaching entertainment as his young wife. She had kept her promise. There was to be no dancing, and none of the gilded youth of Paris had been invited, though Duturque had been besieged by requests for invitations from even the highest quarters. It was to be a fête given to intellect and talent. Beautiful women had been invited, but they were actresses celebrated for genius as well as beauty. The men belonged for the most part to the world of art and letters; but from a list furnished by Perez the world of finance had also been bidden to the fête, and the Bourse would be represented by its most powerful members.

Madame Quijada had been allowed no active part in the preparation of her daughter's first party; but she expressed herself gratified that the gloomy spell was about to be lifted from the house. Louise Marcet assisted in all the floral decorations, for in the arrangement of flowers her taste was unerring; but she told her cousin that she should not appear at the party.

"I should be like the skeleton at an Egyptian banquet," she said, when Dolores pressed her to share in the amusement of the evening. "It would make people melancholy to see so gloomy a figure."

"Poor old Louise," murmured Dolores, moved to pity by the thought of this blighted life, for which even pleasure had no charm, novelty no fascination; "your misfortunes must have been very terrible to deaden all your delight in life, to make you so different from other women."

"My misfortunes were not of a common kind, Dolores. If you knew all, you would hardly wonder that I stand alone with the memory of my grief."

"But you have never trusted me with the secrets of your girlhood; you have never confided in me," said Dolores, reproachfully. "Though we are cousins, I know no more about the cause of the illness that changed you than if we were strangers."

"There are some secrets that must be kept— secrets that involve the fate of other people."

"Well, I have never tormented you with questions; I am only sorry to see you unhappy."

"I am used to bearing my own burden, Dolores; and I am very glad to see you so much happier than you used to be."

"Oh, I have made up my mind to make the best of my life, if Perez will only be reasonable, and allow me my own way. I was simply breaking my heart in the Rue St. Guillaume for want of something to do and to think about. I used to read of balls and parties, of all the grand entertainments of Paris, and the gowns and the jewels, while I was sitting solitary, with my diamonds locked up in their cases. And then, as for the rest," with a sigh, "there's no use in crying for the moon, is there, Louise? When one has not what one loves, one must love what one has."

"If you are thinking of Leon Duverdier, I can tell you that he is not worth one regret," said Louise, earnestly. "Try to forget that you ever saw his face."

"I have been trying ever since I married my good old Perez. Yes; you are right, Louise. He is not worth one regretful thought. He never cared for me, and I was a fool ever to care for him."

"He never cared for any living creature except himself, Dolores. His heart is harder than the nethermost millstone."

CHAPTER VIII.

THE ROC'S EGG.

IT was within an hour of the dinner party which was to precede Madame Perez's reception, and Dolores was sitting before her dressing-table, while the most fashionable hairdresser in Paris brushed and divided the long tresses of raven hair before building them up after the latest invention of his genius.

"Remember, Monsieur Jeck, my coiffure is to be Oriental—all that there is of the most Oriental," said Dolores, decisively.

M. Jeck shrugged his shoulders despondently. All his inventive and imitative powers had of late been concentrated upon the school of Pompadour and Du Barry. His delight had been to pile a coiffure as high as art, horse-

hair, and hair-pins could raise the human hair.
If he had taken any step in another direction, it
would have been a retrograde step. He would
have gone back to the Montespan and the
Fontanges period, which was also an elevated
school. But the Oriental, the school of drooping
tresses and long plaits, the school which must
needs restrict its operations to the hair that grew
on the head of the subject, and could borrow
nothing from art !

True, that in the subject now under his hands
there was abundant material for artistic treat-
ment, but the Oriental style offered no scope for
the caprices of genius.

"Has Madame made up her mind irrevocably ? "
asked the hairdresser.

"Yes, yes, I tell you. My costume is
Oriental."

"Then I have only to submit ; but I must
warn Madame that the Eastern style—the style
of Rebecca of York—is not that which will most
set off Madame's beauty."

"I detest Rebecca of York. Make me a

coiffure à la Roxalane. Something light and gay. I don't want to look a tragedy queen."

"Has Madame any diamond crescents among her jewels?"

"As many as you like. Rosalie, bring me the case of crescents."

The lady's maid brought a large purple velvet jewel-case, which he placed open on the marble-dressing-table. There were crescents of diamonds and rubies, diamonds and sapphires, diamonds and emeralds, diamonds pure and simple.

"Ciel!" cried the coiffeur; "I see my way to a startling success."

He wove the soft black hair into three long plaits, and bound them round the small head in a triple coronet, and into this crown of plaited hair he stuck the jewelled crescents with an inimitable taste and lightness, until the dark hair served only as the background to a blaze of jewels.

"Yes, that will do," said Dolores, surveying herself in her hand-glass. "That will do very well for the Princess Badroulbadour."

"I could have pleased myself better had

Madame given me greater liberty," said M. Jeck, sighing as he folded his apron.

"You have pleased me, and that is more to the point," replied Dolores, with the air of a duchess, scarcely deigning to acknowledge the hairdresser's departing salutation.

Half an hour later her toilette was complete, and she went down to the morning-room, where she was to receive her husband's guests, the drawing-room being transformed for the evening reception.

Her Badroulbadour gown was of palest rose brocade, falling in long straight folds from the shoulders, clasped across the bust with a splendid heart-shaped emerald, and opening over a white satin petticoat, embroidered with an artful and artistic admixture of beetles' wings and emeralds. To the superficial observer that glittering green embroidery looked one mass of emeralds, and seemed to represent wealth even greater than Perez Peru could command.

The millionaire gazed at his wife in a stupor of admiration.

"Dolores, why on earth have you put on all that splendour?" he exclaimed. "I have always understood that it is bad taste for a hostess to be finer than her guests."

"Nobody cares for good or bad taste under the Republic," answered Dolores. "I want people to talk about my dress, and for that one must be splendid and original. My fête to-night is to be a scene out of the Arabian Nights. Do you think I look like the Princess Badroulbadour?"

"You look very lovely," said Perez, who had never heard of Aladdin's wife.

"And you are proud of me, and that is all I want," answered Dolores, caressingly. "Your human-ingots can appear as soon as they please. Ah, here comes mother."

Madame Quijada had shown no aspiring after originality in her toilet, but she was richly dressed in black brocade and diamonds, with a Spanish mantilla of valuable old lace, a costume which became her severe style of countenance better than any more brilliant toilet would have

done.   She was looking ill, and that calm dignity
which had distinguished her appearance in the
seclusion of the Rue St. Guillaume had given
place to a nervous and sometimes restless manner,
which a medical man would at once have
recognized as the manner of a sufferer from
alcoholic poisoning in some form or other.

"I hope you are satisfied at last, madame,"
said her son-in-law; "all Paris is coming to see
what a fool an old man can make of himself for
the sake of a pretty woman."

"If the woman is only pretty enough, all Paris
will go away convinced of your good sense,"
retorted Dolores, gaily.

M. and Madame Joffroy were announced in the
next minute, and Dolores showed the most
amiable *empressement* in receiving a tall, gaunt
personage in sapphire velvet and rubies, who
twenty years earlier had been the cynosure of a
drinking cellar in the vicinity of the Boulevard
St. Michel, and who was now the discontented
wife of one of the richest men in Paris.

More guests arrived.   Herr Hausroth and his

daughters, young ladies who gave themselves tremendous airs on the strength of their father's wealth, and who were rendered miserable by their father's shabby coats, and by certain little miserly eccentricities of which he could not divest himself, although living in princely style and allowing his girls to get their gowns from the most expensive *faiseur* in Paris, which meant a corresponding expensiveness in all the minor details of their toilet, the great *faiseur* taking the word "Thorough" for his motto, and insisting upon his clients striving after ideal perfection in the art of dress. "A badly cut corset, or a hair's breadth too much thickness in a petticoat will spoil my finest conception," said the great *faiseur*.

Two more financiers appeared, these without womankind, and in the little bustle and talk which followed upon their entrance, Madame Quijada drew her daughter aside.

"He is in Paris," she whispered.

"Not Leon?" questioned Dolores, nervously.

"Yes, Leon. I received a letter from him just now, while I was dressing."

"I wish never to see him again."

"But he is coming to your party to-night. You must receive him civilly."

"He has no business to invite himself to my party—after leaving Paris without a word of adieu—and never writing to us in all these months."

"He is your cousin. He heard of your party from strangers, and it was scarcely strange he should invite himself. You must be civil to him, Dolores. You were only too fond of him once. You can at least afford to be polite and friendly to him to-night."

"I won't be uncivil," answered Dolores, moodily, "but I wish he were not coming. I don't want him to cross my threshold."

Her face had clouded over, all the girlish gaiety had gone from her manner, as she took M. Joffroy's arm and led the way into the dining-room, where the arrangement of table, flowers, and lighting was exquisite.

All her pleasure in the prospect of the evening's triumph was damped by the return of this

man, whose coming had once been looked forward
to with feverish impatience, whose absence had
made the world seem a blank. She had had
much time for quiet thought since her marriage
with Pedro Perez, and her whole nature had
changed for the better since her position had
been legitimated, and she was able to look
society straight in the face. Her heart was
young enough and warm enough to be touched
by an old man's affection ; and now that she no
longer considered herself a prisoner and a slave,
she felt sincerely grateful to her millionaire
husband.

Disenchantment had slowly followed upon
Leon's prolonged absence. She had begun to
question the merits of the man she had admired,
and whose misfortunes had appealed to her pity.
Little by little she began to see the charlatan
where she had seen the genius, and the cold-
hearted adventurer where she had imagined
the careless, happy-go-lucky student, whose difficulties were a natural result of the artistic temperament.

She had looked back on her intercourse with
her cousin, looked back with unprejudiced eyes,
and she had seen that his conduct had been
mercenary from first to last; that he had taken
every advantage of her regard for him, and had
given her not one token of affection in return.
He had extorted money from her upon every
possible pretence, and he had looked with a
greedy eye upon her jewels, and would gladly
have appropriated them to his own use.

She did not wish ever to see him again, and
she dreaded any encounter between him and
Pedro Perez. His presence at her reception
to-night would be the snake among the flowers.

As the evening went on, however, she tried to
banish all thought about this unbidden guest.
He would only be one among many, she told herself. She could dismiss him with a word.

The dinner seemed a slow business to the
women of the party, but the financiers enjoyed
themselves, and were unanimous in their approval
of the *menu*. Joffroy told his old friend Perez
that he had the prettiest wife and the best cook

in Paris. Hausroth was green with envy, and the daughters Hausroth sniggered together at Madame Perez Peru's Oriental costume, although their own famous *faiseur* had so cleverly planned the gown that it offered no marked eccentricity of character, and might have been worn at a ball at the Elysée.

At ten o'clock Madame Perez was stationed in the drawing-room at the entrance to the marquee, where the electric lamps were artfully dotted about amidst the tropical foliage. The light here and in the adjoining tent was subdued in tone, so that when at the stroke of midnight the velvet curtains of the supper tent were drawn back the roc's egg lamp might burst upon the spectators with overpowering brilliance.

The roc's egg was the one feature of the party with which Dolores hoped to startle the spoiled children of Paris.

The two tents for conversation and music filled quickly. Everybody had flocked eagerly to see the beautiful Madame Perez. A curious mingling of the *grand monde* and the *demi-monde* was to be noted among the guests—a new feature in the life of great cities, and an evidence of the march of progress. Great ladies had begged for invitations which had been intended only for actresses and for the wives and daughters of artists with pen or pencil. Ducal coronets were on some of the carriages which were waiting yonder in the wintry darkness of the wood. Dukes and Duchesses had declared that they only wanted to " look in " at the millionaire's party, only to get a glimpse of the millionaire's wife ; but finding the palm-shadowed tent a very agreeable lounge, and that Faure and Capoul, and Albani and Marie Roze, were among the singers, great ladies and their cavaliers lingered, and began even to express a mild curiosity about supper, which some one had said was to be served punctually at midnight.

Leon Duverdier approached his cousin immediately after she had exchanged courtesies with the ancient but beautiful Marquise Talonrouge and the lovely *comédienne*, Clara Beauville. He bore himself with his usual assured and supercilious air, but Dolores noted that he looked pale and ill, and that he was thinner than when she saw him last.

"I congratulate you upon the success of your fête," he said, holding his cousin's hand with a lingering pressure. "All the notabilities of Paris are pouring in at your door. I am glad I returned in the nick of time to assist at your triumph."

"Was it worth while to return at all after you had stayed away so long?" asked Dolores, looking at him with a deliberate disdain which had as chilling an effect as a cold douche after the hot room in a Turkish bath.

"My dear Dolores, matrimony seems to have made a remarkable change in your manner to your own kith and kin," he said, smiling at her. "I hope your head is not going to be turned by social success."

"No, my head will not be turned; but my eyes have been opened. You left Paris without a word to the people who—who cared for you. Can you wonder if they were enlightened by your conduct, and left off caring for one who set so small a value upon the ties of kindred ? I think I have learnt to understand your character during your long absence, and that I know you now almost as well as Louise knows you."

His face darkened at the name, and he looked round the room and beyond into the crowded tent, as if he were searching out an enemy.

"I see," he said. "Louise has been slandering me to you. I will not detain you from your guests; but later you must give me a few minutes' quiet conversation. I have something important to say to you. It is a matter of life and death."

"I recognize the old prelude," said Dolores; "*question d'argent*."

Leon Duverdier moved onward, into the tent where people were promenading amidst a Babel of talk, and to the tent beyond, where Capoul was singing the "Alléluia d'amour."

Yes, the party was a success; and walking about quietly among people who were for the most part strangers to him, Pedro Perez was gratified by overhearing enthusiastic praises of his wife's grace and beauty, her jewels, her costume, and the originality of her reception. True, that he heard more than one witticism at his own expense, and was reminded of a fact which he had never ignored—the fact that he was old, and plain, and insignificant, and that his only value in the eyes of the houri in blush-rose satin and many-coloured gems must needs lie in his millions. He heard, and he did not despair. There was something—an undefinable change in Dolores—which told him she was not altogether ungrateful; and he thought that if he could pension off Madame Quijada and have his young wife all to himself, free from the mother's sinister influence, there would not be a happier husband in all Paris than he, Perez Peru. As for those airy shafts of ridicule which he had so dreaded in the past, he was resigned to endure them in the future, so long as all went well in his domestic life.

The concert closed with *éclat* in a new part-song, composed by Monsieur Duturque, who had

adroitly converted to his own use a certain almost
forgotten march in an opera by Lulli, a stirring
melody which put the audience in good humour;
and with the last chord the velvet curtains which
concealed the supper tent were drawn suddenly
apart, and the roc's egg lamp bathed the scene in
a soft, yet dazzling light, which set off the vivid
colouring of fruit and flowers, silver-gilt, and
Venetian glass, saumon à la Chambord, and
homard en aspic, on the fifty supper tables.

There was a lively chorus of approval from the
guests, who had been wondering where the supper
was to come from, and whether they were going
to be put off with tea and coffee, ices, and iced
drinks at the buffet in the dining-room. The
fifty tables were occupied as if by magic, and two
hundred and odd tongues were chattering about
the roc's egg.

" *Quelle belle idée! Mais c'est une féerie. Il n'y
a que l'argent pour faire des merveilles. C'est la
baguette de la Bourse*——" and so on, and so on,
with illimitable variations upon the same theme.

The supper tables were occupied till nearly two

o'clock, and there was no failure in the supplies. At two, everybody had supped, and almost everybody had departed, save a few night-bird journalists, who still sat drinking and talking at a couple of tables. Among these was Leon Duverdier.

As the clock struck two, the roc's egg lamp was extinguished, and the curtains fell, leaving the lingering guests in total darkness.

"I call that about the broadest hint our fair hostess could give us," said the editor of a famous Parisian paper; and there was a good deal of talk and laughter from the Bohemian band during some minutes of darkness, at the end of which interval the curtains were drawn back again by invisible hands, and the last guests strolled through the empty tents to the drawing-room, where Dolores was waiting to bid good night, with the faithful Duturques to keep her company. Madame Quijada had retired within the last hour, and Pedro Perez had sneaked off to his own apartment soon after the opening of the supper-room.

The editor of the *Guerre aux Sots* was full of apologies.

"That is the worst of the brotherhood of letters," he said gaily; "we are so fond of one another's society that it is much easier to assemble than to disperse us. Besides, who would be in a hurry to leave fairyland? If it had not been for the sportiveness of the roc's egg we should have lingered till the sun put that emblem of magic power to shame."

"I am sorry the lamp behaved so badly," said Dolores, with an arch smile.

"Ah, madame, was there not a fairy in league with the lamp, a benevolent fairy, who knows that we are hardworking journalists, who can but snatch a few hours' rest between the tail of to-day's epigram and the head of to-morrow's, and that we need the quiet of the night to elaborate the impromptus of the day."

"I must apologize for my husband, gentlemen," said Dolores. "He is not used to evening parties, so he stole away soon after midnight, leaving my mother and me to represent him."

"Jupiter need not apologize for retiring to his tent of clouds when he leaves Juno and Venus in his place," said the youngest of the scribblers; and then each made his farewell bow, till all were gone except Leon.

He lingered, with a determined air, even after the Duturques had bade good night, the pianiste rapturous at the success of *our* party.

CHAPTER IX.

CRUEL AS THE GRAVE.

LEON DUVERDIER and his cousin were alone in
the drawing-room. Through the draped opening
of the large central window the dimly lighted
marquee loomed shadowy, and the tropical
foliage had a sombre air. The fountain had
left off playing, the electric light had been
turned off in all three tents, and the long vista
of palms, and flowers, and tapestry, and velvet-
curtained archways took a funereal aspect,
lighted only by a few small clusters of wax
candles placed here and there amidst the foliage.

Dolores looked at her cousin, stifled a yawn,
and walked slowly towards the bell beside the
chimney-piece.

"I am sure you don't expect me to be inclined

for conversation at this late hour, Leon," she said coldly; "so, if you'll allow me, I'll order your carriage."

"Please don't take that useless trouble. I have no carriage. I came in a cab, and dismissed it. I shall walk back to my hotel."

"You are not at your old address?"

"No; I am staying at the Hotel St. Lazare for a night or two. I am only in Paris as a bird of passage. I sail next week from Havre—for Buenos Ayres."

"I hope you will be more fortunate there than you appear to have been here," said Dolores, calmly.

He was dumfounded by the coolness of her reply. Could so brief a separation have worked such a change in the woman who only a few few months ago had obviously adored him? He was silent for some moments. The tone of his reply was constrained.

"I congratulate you on the wisdom of your course since I left Paris," he said; "you have only followed my advice. I often told you that

Perez was devoted enough to marry you, if you played your cards properly."

"Yes; he is devoted, which is strange—and I am grateful, which may seem even more extraordinary."

"And you are happy, I suppose?"

"Yes, I am actually happy; but I hardly realized till to-night how pleasant it is to be the wife of a millionaire."

"I am glad you have found out the value of wealth—and that your experience has been on the sunny side of the question, and not its dark side. I know the value of money from the lack of it—but I am now on a sure road to fortune. I have a better chance and a finer opening in Brazil than I ever had in my life——"

"I congratulate you," said Dolores.

"But I cannot grasp this golden opportunity without a certain capital in hand. Money makes money, Dolores. A man must sow the golden seed—if only a handful of gold dust—before he can reap the golden harvest. Fortune is at my door, if I can let her in; but I must first find the key that will open the door."

"Your conversation really abounds in allegories," replied Dolores; "but though the variations are new, the tune is always the same. No, Leon, I cannot provide you with the capital for your Brazilian venture. I mean to be a loyal wife to Pedro Perez, and I will do nothing underhand or secret—nothing that could awaken one jealous doubt in his mind. I know enough of his character to know that with him jealousy would be terrible."

"Then you will do nothing for me? You are wallowing in wealth, and you will not lift your finger to help me?"

"Oh yes, I will do much more than lift my finger. Your new venture is to be made in South America, where my husband is a power. He knows every inch of the country—every speculation and enterprise that has been made there. I will introduce your scheme to him, and ask him to help you."

"And you think he will help me?"

"Yes, when I plead for you."

"I cannot wait for such a slow process as that, Dolores. I know what these old men are, and how long they deliberate before they will trust a young man with a thousand pounds sterling, even if he could buy the philosopher's stone for the money, and offered to share the profits of the transaction. I want money at once, Dolores. Can't you understand that two or three hundred pounds to-night would be worth a thousand next week? And I know you must have as much as that."

"I have not the tenth part of two hundred pounds," answered his cousin, coolly. "I have everything in the world I can wish for, but since I have been Pedro's wife I have had hardly any money. I am Madame Perez. The name is enough. I can order anything I want from any tradesman in Paris, and my name is all I need give in exchange. Pedro pays my bills as fast as they come in. I have nothing to do with money; so you see, if I were ever so willing to help you, I couldn't do it."

There was a pause, during which the man who called himself Leon Duverdier took two or three turns up and down the room, in troubled meditation. Then he stopped suddenly, and confronted Dolores with a frowning brow.

"It is mere idle sophistication to talk to me in this strain," he said. "You can help me, if you like, and you know it. If you have not bank-notes or gold you have money's worth. You have jewels which I could turn into immediate cash at the Mont de Piété. I only ask for the loan of a few of your gewgaws, those you value least, that I may raise money upon them for a month or so. I will remit the money to a friend in Paris as soon as I am in funds; and the jewels shall be safely delivered into your own hands, at the hour and place which you yourself shall appoint. Will that do for you?"

"No, it will not. I will not trust you with one of my husband's gifts—indeed, I dare not. Pedro remembers every jewel he ever gave me, and asks me from time to time to wear particular ornaments. I should be disgraced if I could not comply with his request."

The argument which followed was long and angry. Leon grew desperate as he found Dolores firm in her refusal.

"You had better not goad me too far," he hissed in her ear, as she shrank from him, with her back against the angle of the low marble mantelpiece, and her hand stretched towards the bell. "It is a very small thing I have asked of you. Yet the consequences of your refusal may be more disastrous than you can foresee. I may be tempted to throw up the sponge, and to let the world know some secrets in my life, and your mother's share in them. That revelation would be a worse disgrace for you than the loss of a diamond necklace."

He was gone, leaving Dolores mystified by his parting words, but not greatly alarmed. It seemed to her that those words were an idle threat; and that all she had to do was to stand firm in her duty to her husband, who was powerful enough to protect her from her kinsman's malice. There was nothing in her past relations with Leon which could bring evil to her in the future. She had loved him with a sentimental girlish fancy, which had been fostered by the monotony of her secluded existence. Now that she had begun to taste the sweets of life, and to understand the omnipotence of wealth, she looked back and wondered at her girlhood's idle fancy.

"How could I have ever been blind to his selfishness and meanness?" she wondered, when the outer door had closed upon her cousin.

It was four o'clock upon a winter morning. The last faint glow had faded out of the logs, and Dolores shivered in her splendour, as she surveyed her dazzling image in the vast sheet of glass behind a low jardinière filled with hyacinths and narcissus. The image which met her gaze was radiant with gems and brilliant colouring, but the face under the jewelled turban was pale and weary.

"It has been a long, long night," she thought, "but at last I have made my début in Parisian

society.   Perez Peru's wife is no longer a person
to be hidden in an obscure lodging."

The servants, who had been supping luxu-
riously in their own quarters, now appeared,
sober and serious of aspect, apparently intent
upon the safe adjustment of locks and bolts, and
the putting away of stray valuables. The last
glimmer of light had been extinguished in the
marquees, and to-morrow morning all that fairy
scene would be taken to pieces, like a child's
puzzle, and carted away, while the roc's egg
lamp would be sold at a sacrifice to some enter-
prising proprietor of café or music-hall.

The footman drew aside the plush curtains,
and shut the wide plate-glass window, which
fastened in the usual manner of French case-
ments ; and it may be that under the influence
of trufiled turkey and champagne he was somewhat uncertain in twisting the long brass bolt
into its socket.

" Is all safe ? " asked Dolores, listlessly, as she
took up her ostrich fan and moved slowly
towards the door.

" Yes, Madame."

" Then you may go to bed, all of you."

" Madame will require the services of Elise at her toilette ? "

" Not to-night. Tell her to bring me my chocolate at ten to-morrow morning, and on no account to disturb me before that hour."

Now that the tension of supreme excitement was relaxed Dolores felt tired to death. She had been moving about among her guests, and talking, and laughing at every sally of wit or journalist, artist or actor, for five mortal hours; to say nothing of those three quieter hours during which she had presided at her husband's dinner-party. She could hardly crawl upstairs to her luxurious bedroom, and she was far too weary to submit to the somewhat oppressive attentions of a highly trained lady's maid—a maid who had lived but lately with haggard old age, which required to be put together bit by bit, and composed and painted into a ghastly semblance of youth and beauty. She had but just strength to unclasp her jewels—her necklace

of matchless pearls, the stars and clusters and
hearts and horseshoes of diamonds, emeralds,
and sapphires which studded her bodice, the
crescents which flashed from her dark hair. She
was just able to take off all these splendours, and
to drop them in a careless heap upon her
dressing-table; and then she exchanged her
silken garment for a loose muslin peignoir, threw
back the satin-covered eider-down, and flung
herself upon her bed, overcome with sleep.

All was still upon that upper floor. Pedro
Perez was sleeping the tranquil slumber of the
man who knows that all his investments are safe,
and that some of them are yielding him fifteen
per cent.; Madame Quijada was sleeping the
heavy sleep of senses stupefied by chloral; the
servants had crept up to their attics in the
Italian roof—that these cubicula were cold in
winter and hot in summer had but little disturbed the repose of the architect who planned
the villa;—and on all eyelids in the house sleep
lay heavy, save in that one modest chamber
where Louise Marcet lay in her narrow bed, and

turned upon her pillow from time to time in the
long intervals between her brief slumbers. The
time was when the tired work-girl's night had
been a night of a single sleep; but since that
malady in which reason had been nearly wrecked
in the agonized brain, Louise had never known
what it was to enjoy long and tranquil slumbers.
To-night her nerves had been shaken by the noises
within and without the house, the din of talk and
laughter, the rattle of silver and glass, the loud
music of a brass band playing waltzes and
mazurkas, the sound of singing, and the roll of
carriage-wheels. Gaiety of this kind had lost
all fascination for her. She had never tasted
such pleasures; and she had no curiosity about
that brilliant world of the rich and well-born in
which she had had no part. Her day of happiness had been as brief as a butterfly's summer;
her pleasures had been of the simplest. She
had known the passion of love only in its most
ideal aspect. She had never been sickened by
the reverse of the picture. The man she had
exalted into a hero had been her hero to the

end of his life; and her regret for him was so much the keener that she had never had cause to doubt his honour or his worthiness to be loved. Thus the girl's innocent love of a summer day had become the settled worship of a lost lover; and the woman's heart was dead to all but the broken dream of the love-sick girl.

Darkness closed round the villa in the Bois, in those chill hours between night and morning,—bitter cold in the garden outside, but tempered within these walls by the *calorifère* in the basement. There were only two lamps burning in the house — one, the coloured glass lantern in the hall, where the lowered gas gave a subdued glimmer that made the shadows blacker on the staircase and landing; the other, the little antique silver lamp that hung above the bed where Dolores lay in the happy sleep of youth and health, and a heart at ease.

Not a sound in that sleeping household, save the striking of various clocks, with more or less

musical chime. Five o'clock! Yes, there is
another sound. As the hammer falls on the
gong for the fifth time, there is the sound of a
window opening softly and slowly on the ground
floor—then a pause; and then the cautious
opening of a door—another pause; and again
another sound—the stealthy tread of lightly-shod
feet on the velvet pile of the staircase.

Louise Marcet hears those sounds faintly in
her sleep. Are the servants going down already?
It is early for them, considering the lateness of
the hour at which they went to rest. She is
sleeping somewhat more deeply than usual, worn
out by the noises that kept her awake till an
hour or so ago. It is her habit to rise when the
servants go down in the morning, to be as early
as the earliest of the household, and to see that
the day's work is begun betimes; but this
morning her senses are dull, she mixes the
sounds of those footsteps with a confused dream
of the past. It is a summer Sunday morning,
and her kindly neighbour is coming to call her,
that she may be up and dressed and away to the

station of St. Lazare, to meet the kindly
Englishman, for that promised excursion to
Marley le Roi.

Fond dream of days long vanished. Fancy
bridges the dismal gulf of years, and the grave
where her lover lies; and she hears his voice
and sees his face again, just as she heard and
saw him more than twenty years ago.

Suddenly the face fades, the voice is silent.
She starts up in her bed shuddering, her blood
turned to ice at the sound of a woman's shriek—
either of fear or pain. She springs from her bed,
throws on the peignoir that lies ready in the
chair close by, and moves out to the landing, and
to her cousin's room. The door is open, and in
the dim light of the night-lamp she sees a white
figure lying on the carpet, face downwards, and,
standing by the dressing-table, she sees her
brother engaged in thrusting the heaped-up
jewels into his pockets. While she pauses in the
doorway, transfixed, he crams the last of the
ornaments out of sight, and turns to leave the
room, without one glance at the prostrate form

near the bed. He recoils with an angry oath at the sigh of Louise.

"Stand out of the way," he says savagely, "or I'll settle you as I've settled her."

"Thief—murderer."

"Bosh! She's only stunned. It'll be worse for you than for her if you don't hold your tongue. Let me pass, I say."

"Not with those jewels in your possession," she says, facing him fearlessly.

Before he can prevent her she has locked the door and put the key in her pocket.

"Thief and murderer—your first crime has gone unpunished because my voice has not been lifted up against you—but there shall be no second crime that I can hinder. I am trusted in this house, and I mean to protect my cousin's property. If you have killed her, your life shall pay for hers. You shall not leave this room till you have given up those jewels, and until I see if she is living or dead."

She moves towards the figure on the ground, and as she does so he looks round and grasps the situation. There is no other way out of the room. The only other door stands wide open revealing the interior of a bath-room in which there is no door—only a great marble bath and white panelled walls. He grasps Louise by the shoulder, and snatches the key from the wide pocket of her dressing-gown.

"Stand aside, and keep a quiet tongue in your head," he whispers threateningly; and then as she clings about him, clutching the collar of his coat, holding him with all the force of excitement that has reached fever pitch, he sees her head flung back and her lips parting in a cry for help. Another instant and she will raise the house. A cruel blow from his clenched hand stifles the cry upon her whitening lips, and then the same deadly hand snatches a knife from his breast pocket, a knife that opens with a spring.

A thrust, and another, and then he grows mad with rage, the blind unreasoning fury of a savage beast, as the lips still strive to cry aloud, and the eyes still stare at him wildly, and the clinging hands still hold him, and so another, and yet another thrust of the murderous knife, till one last gurgling sound escapes from those distorted lips, the stare grows fixed and dull, the fingers loosen, and the bleeding form falls at his feet.

He unlocks the door and runs downstairs, splashed with her blood, a sister's life blood, and creeps out by the way he came in, stealing through the empty tents, spurning the fading flowers, as he dashes out into the cold night, through the silken draperies that mark an opening in the canvas.

He did not mean murder when he entered the house, least of all a sister's murder; but he meant plunder, and he has secured the booty. At daybreak he will leave for Dunkirk; from Dunkirk to Holland, where he will dispose of the gems, minus their delicate Tiffany settings.

Just at the last moment he remembers that he must hide the blood upon his clothes. The stains are darkest and biggest upon his shirt and waistcoat, as his victim clung about him in the death-struggle.

He creeps back into the house, finds some

overcoats hanging in a vestibule, and takes an
Inverness, which is just long enough to hide his
figure to the knees.

This precaution is unlucky, for in going out
into the garden he falls into the arms of a gendarme, who, riding quietly by in the night
silence, had noticed the opening of the little
door in the marquee. The gendarme dismounts,
and waits to see who will emerge from that mysterious little door at a quarter-past five in the
morning.

And so Leon Duverdier, *alias* Claude Morel,
falls into the clutches of the law, and is shut up
au secret in a felon's cell, to be taken out at
intervals and interrogated by the *Juge d'Instruction;* and before night all Paris knows that
there has been a daring robbery and a brutal
murder in Perez Peru's villa, that the beautiful
Madame Perez has been struck to the ground
senseless in the attempt to protect her matchless
jewels from a burglar, and lies in a precarious
condition, and that poor old Perez is half mad
with grief and anxiety.

CHAPTER X.

IT is almost a month since I last opened this book, a month which has brought me daily nearer and nearer in union with him who is to share all my life, and whom I am to love and obey. Yes, obey; the word suggests not the faintest sense of humiliation. I am proud to have a master, such a master. I never had that kind of feeling with my poor dear Cyril. On the contrary, I felt as if he had been given to me as my slave, a person to order about.

For the first few days after that terrible revelation about my step-father I kept my ghastly secret. I could not trust even him whom I had trusted with my whole heart and my whole life. I feared that if I told Gilbert my conviction of Ambrose Arden's guilt; if I

showed him how link by link the chain of circumstantial evidence could be put together until
the circle was complete, he might consider it his
duty to bring about a public investigation, and
thus condemn my mother to the horror of knowing what manner of man she had married. But
after torturing myself for those few days of
puzzled thought and nights of feverish unrest, I
could bear my burden no longer. Gilbert saw
that there was something amiss with me, that
even his presence could not make me happy, and
he urged me to confide in him. And so I told
him all the dismal story, and my reasons for
believing that my father's murder had been
plotted by his friend.

I could see by his darkening countenance as
he listened that he was of my opinion; but he
answered gravely and deliberately—

"Your theory is plausible, Daisy, yet there is
no incident in life which may not bear a double
interpretation. I certainly believe Duverdier to
be the murderer, as surely as I believe him to be
Claude Morel under another name; and granting

that he is the guilty man, it is assuredly a
strange thing that he should dog your step-
father's footsteps in this quiet place, and that
your lover should renounce the happiness of his
life, and go into exile, after overhearing a
conversation between his father and that man.
The links are strong links; but the evidence is
not of a kind that would be accepted in a court
of law; and I doubt if the law will ever touch
the man whose moral guilt, granting him guilty,
is greater than the guilt of the shedder of blood."

"I don't want the law to touch him; I don't
want my mother ever to know how cruelly she
has been cheated and deceived. I only want you
to understand the horror of it all; and that this
man with whom I have to live in daily friendship, or the appearance of friendship, is of all
men upon earth the most abhorrent to me."

Half the weight of my burden was lifted off
my shoulders after I had shared my trouble with
Gilbert. He is so wise, so thoughtful, so just,
and temperate in his judgments. He would not
allow that the case was established against that

wretched man. It was a case for grave doubt,
he told me. The circumstances were full of
darkest suspicion; but it would be dangerous
to condemn a fellow-creature, above all a friend
to whom I owed so much, upon such evidence.

I shuddered at the word "friend."

"Oh, I was so fond of him once," I said. "I
used to sit upon his knee and put my arms
round his neck. I called him uncle because I
could not bear to think that he was not related
to me. I used to run from my father to him,
and one was almost as dear to me as the other.
And now to know that he is utterly base, false,
and cruel, inexorably cruel, cruel as death
itself!"

"We know nothing, Daisy," said my dearest,
in his calm, grave voice; "there is nothing
absolute or conclusive in all your evidence. The
signs of trouble of mind which you have noticed
in your step-father may be only the indications
of physical disease. We must wait, and watch,
if need be, and whether this dire suspicion of
yours be brought more fully home to us, or

whether we have reason to doubt the grounds upon which it rests, there is at least one point upon which we can have no hesitation : the knowledge of evil must be kept from your mother."

I was inexpressibly comforted by his counsel, and felt that I could better endure to live in the same house with my step-father. I even began to falter somewhat in my judgment of him; and had it not been for the mystery of Cyril's conduct, which I could account for in no other manner, I might have thought myself the victim of a delusion, cruel alike to me and to the man whom I suspected.

But I could not forget the evidence of Cyril's face, which told of dire calamity, or the stern resolve with which he cancelled the bond between us. His tone and manner were those of a man who was fulfilling a painful duty, who submitted himself to a cruel destiny.

Nor was there other and nearer evidence wanting in my step-father's manner to me after the change in my manner to him, which must have been obvious, although I set a watch upon

myself always in my mother's presence. On the
rare occasions when Mr. Arden and I were alone
together, I maintained a resolute silence, and on
no such occasion did he ever question me as to
my altered bearing. It seemed to me that he
submitted to our estrangement as a part of his
doom, and that he tacitly accepted my condemnation of him. Not by one word or look
did he ever seek to evoke the old tenderness of
our relations. He who until a few weeks ago
had been to me as a second father was content
to become a stranger, and to endure the insult
of my sullen silence; content also to play the
hypocrite in his wife's presence, and to affect that
he and I were on the old affectionate terms.
When mother asked me to play to him he
praised my playing, and asked for this or that
sonata or set of variations. Oh, what a dreadful
life it would be if it were not for the comfort
and support my true lover has given me throughout this trial!

And all this time there has been an air of

gaiety at River Lawn, and mother and Gilbert and I have been full of preparations for the great change in our lives. It will not be such a change for mother and me, though, as it might have been under less blessed conditions; for I shall be her next-door neighbour, and shall be running in and out of the dear home garden every day, and she can run into my gardens, and the ever lovely and beloved arbour where my sovereign lord and king first declared his love can be common ground for both of us. I shall keep copies of my most adorable poets there, and a sketching block and colour-box, and Gilbert shall have a box of cigars or cigarettes in the handy little cupboard where I used to keep my toy cups and saucers when I was a child.

No; my wedding-day will bring no severance between mother and me; and by-and-by, when the end which I foresee shall come, and the shadow is lifted from her life, I shall have that dear mother all to myself again, as I had in the tranquil years of her widowhood.

It is wicked, perhaps, to take comfort in the

thought of any one's death: yet can I wish a traitor's life to be prolonged? Can I fail to see the hand of God in that gradual darkening of the gloom which encircles him—the gradual working of that slow poison we call remorse?

Again there has been talk of my trousseau, and this time mother has not found me cold or indifferent. I have taken a keen delight in everything, especially the house-linen, about which I am as earnest as if I had spun it my-self, like an industrious Swedish or Norwegian maiden, and had hoarded it in great oaken presses to await my betrothal. I am delighted to say that Gilbert's hereditary linen closet exhibits a vast collection of rags, beautiful Irish damask table-cloths, with the Florestan coat-of-arms woven in the fabric, smooth and lustrous as satin, but as transparent as gauze when the good old housekeeper held them up to the light.

"Single gentlemen never do think of such things," she said apologetically; "I've told Mr. Florestan often and often that new table-cloths were wanted, but he always forgot to order them; and then he was here so seldom, and that made him careless about the house."

"Of course," cried I; "what should he know about table-cloths?"

And then mother and I held a grand consultation, and selected the loveliest patterns, and sent off a big order to a firm in Belfast, and I felt that I was encouraging the manufactures of the Sister Isle. There are Irish poplins in my trousseau, too—soft, lustrous, delicious—warm and substantial wear for my winter honeymoon. Mother thinks of everything—seasons and occasions, comfort and dignity. Without folly or extravagance, my trousseau will be perfect— worthy to be exhibited as an example of sterling British common-sense, as opposed to French frivolity and American ostentation.

We are to go to the South for our honeymoon, but not straight away to fashionable Cannes or cosmopolitan Nice. We are to go first to Bordeaux, and then to Pau and Biarritz, and afterwards to Toulouse, Carcassonne, Nismes, Arles, and so on by easy stages to Marseilles, and thence to Cannes, just to wind up with the Prince of Wales's week, and the dances at the two clubs. I shall be an old married woman by that time, capable of chaperoning my unmarried cousins if they should happen to be at Cannes with my aunt just then. They generally go South in early spring, and leave the doctor to make money in Harley Street.

They all came down to River Lawn last week to congratulate me upon my "promotion," as Flora called it, and they all, aunt included, seem to think I have done a grand thing in getting myself engaged to Gilbert Florestan.

"Not because he is rich," explained Flora, "for measured by our modern necessities he is little better than a pauper, but because he is unmistakably *county*. Your relations need never be ashamed of him."

"*That* is a comfort," said I, enraged at her impertinence; "but I hope you don't suppose I accepted Gilbert in order to gratify my relations, or come up to the requirements of Harley Street. I did not accept him because he is county, and I should have been just as deeply in love with him if he had been a beggar."

"Ah, you may think so, and most engaged girls talk in that style," said Flora; "but I have never heard of anybody in society marrying a beggar since the time of King Cophetua, and no doubt *he* was sorry for it afterwards."

These cousins of mine are the very essence of worldliness, and I seldom stoop to argue about matters of feeling with either of them. They have been on the point of making great matches ever since they were presented, but the business has always stopped short of actuality; and Aunt Emily says that marriage, from a lady's standpoint, will soon become impossible.

"It is easy enough for an only child like you," she said. "Of course *you* are anybody's money; but my poor girls have nothing but their beauty and their accomplishments, and men nowadays are utterly sordid."

This was a speech which would have made me wretched were it possible for me to doubt my true lover; but all the discontented mothers in

England might hint and insinuate for a livelong summer day without ruffling my great content. My heart, so far as Gilbert is concerned, is as placid as a summer lake encircled by mountains.

CHAPTER XL

THIS morning the question was mooted, Who was to give me away? It was just as breakfast was over, and Mr. Arden had not yet gone off to his hermitage on the other side of the lane.

"Your step-father is, of course, the proper person," said my mother, looking at her husband with her sweet, gentle smile, a look I understand so well, a look which means kindliness, esteem, respect, consideration, but which never yet meant love.

"No," I cried hastily; "there is only one person who must give me to my husband, and that person is my mother."

"My dearest, it would be so unusual for a woman——" began mother.

Mr. Arden interrupted her hastily.

VOL. III.   O

"Not in the case of a widow, Clara," he said, in his calm, measured way, as if there were no hint of aversion in my hasty protest. "I agree with Daisy—you are the fittest person to give your daughter to the man of her choice. The act will stamp your approval of the union; and Daisy is wise in wishing that it should be so."

Twice he mentioned me by my old familiar name, without the faintest emotion. No witness of that scene could have suspected from his tone or conduct that there was any gulf between us. I sat with my eyes fixed upon the table-cloth, waiting for him to leave us before I could feel happy or at ease.

It was on the morning after this that the dreadful shock came, and still this man of blood was calm and collected, equal to the occasion.

The newspapers are delivered at River Lawn at about ten o'clock, and on this particular morning we were later than usual at breakfast, and the meal was only just over when Mead brought in his tray of papers ready aired and cut.

My step-father took the *Times*, my mother the *Morning Post*. I am only interested in Mead's tray on the mornings that bring the *World*, *Punch*, or *Truth*; so on Tuesday morning there was nothing to claim my attention, and I sat idly by while the other two read their papers.

An exclamation from my mother startled me from a reverie. "Oh, God!" she cried, rising hurriedly and going over to her husband, with the newspaper in her hand, "it has come, it has come at last. 'Vengeance is mine, I will repay, saith the Lord.' My husband's murderer will be punished—after all these years. Ambrose, do you see, do you know what has happened? Have you read?"

"Have I read what? My dear Clara, are you mad?" he asked, looking up at her wonderingly, as she stood before him, with white cheeks and dilated eyes.

"Have you read the French news? A dreadful murder—the murder of a woman by a man who is supposed to be her brother—by a man called Leon Duverdier, *alias* Claude Morel.

Claude Morel! The man who killed my husband."

"No, I have not seen the French news," he answered slowly.

A lie! The paper lay under his hand as he spoke, and I saw the heading of the column— "Paris. By Telegraph."

"Read, then; read the account of the murder, and of the man. He is in prison. He was caught at once, this time; taken red-handed. The police in Paris are better than the feeble wretches who let my dear love's murderer go scot-free. Read, read, read, Ambrose!"

She was beside herself with agitation. Her husband started to his feet, and put his arm round her and held her to his breast, held her against that false and cruel heart, whose baseness she knew not.

"Control yourself, Clara, for pity's sake. Remember we have no sure ground for believing that Morel was the murderer."

"Yes, yes, we have, conclusive ground. The use of his sister's name to decoy my husband;

that in itself was all-sufficient proof. And now, see, the sister is murdered, brutally, savagely stabbed to death by the same hand."

"If there has been murder done, the murderer will suffer for his crime; and in that case your husband will be avenged."

"No, no; that is not enough. That other, more deliberate crime must be brought home to him. His judges must know what a wretch he is. French juries are so merciful. He will be recommended to mercy. Only the murder of a sister, on the spur of the moment. There will be the plea of extenuating circumstances. But let them know how he lured an unoffending man to a lonely room and killed him in cold blood, for sordid gain, and even a French jury must condemn him to death."

"My dearest, you are talking wildly. A man can only be tried for one crime at a time. If he be acquitted of murdering his sister, he can then be indicted for the murder of Robert Hatrell. You must be calm and patient."

"Let us go to Paris to-night."

"I will go there, if you like, and find out all about the man and his crime. It would be useless for you to go."

"No, no: I want to be there, in the city where the murderer is waiting for his doom."

"My dear Clara, I cannot allow you to travel under such conditions. I would not answer for your reason if you were to go upon such a journey. Nor could you possibly leave your daughter, on the eve of her marriage, upon any such mad errand. Whatever has to be done I will do. I will go to-night, and will remain in Paris until after this man's trial. I will find out who he really is, and if he is identical with the Claude Morel whose sister your husband once admired. You may rely upon me to do everything that is necessary or expedient. Only, for God's sake, be calm, be reasonable. Remember how precious your life and reason are to your daughter and to me. Remember how both trembled in the balance years ago in this house."

My poor dear mother commanded herself by a great effort. I could see how she struggled with

her agitation, how earnestly she strove to be
calm.

"I never thought that the hour of retribution
would come," she said. "Oh, the wretch, the
heartless wretch, to strike a strong man down in
the flower of his years, to cut short so dear a life.
No, I will not talk of him any more, Ambrose,"
she said, in answer to a warning look from her
husband. "I will be calm and patient, and wait
for the end. It is coming, in God's own good
time. You need not be afraid about me. Daisy
and I will stay here quietly while you go to
Paris. And you will send me daily reports.
You will not keep me in the dark——"

"Not for an hour."

They went out of the room together, mother
leaning on his arm, confiding in him and relying
upon him, as if he were the best of men. I was
left alone to think over what had happened, and
to consider how this new phase of our terrible
history was likely to affect the dear mother.

First, I read the account of the murder in the
Times, a brutal murder, the act of a thief and

desperado. I will not sully this book by record-
ing it here, since its only bearing on my life
lies in the fact that this wretch who murdered
his sister in a villa in the Bois de Boulogne the
night before last, is in all probability the wretch
who killed my father. I read the savage history,
and then I thought, and thought, and thought;
but I only felt so much the more hopeless and
miserable; and I saw how futile it was for me to
think alone, while the other half of me was not
at my side, to help me out of every difficulty.
So I just ran into the lobby, put on my hat, and
went out into the garden to see if I could find
my dearest and best, who would be able to give
me wise counsel, and whose very voice would
enable me to keep up my courage, were I
hemmed round by difficulties.

It is wintry weather everywhere in this last
month of the year, but our gardens are so rich
in conifers, laurel, and arbutus that they never
look bare or cold; and the shrubbery is so
sheltered by deodar and cupressus, that an
invalid might walk there even on the coldest

morning. I knew it was Gilbert's habit to smoke his after-breakfast cigarette on the other side of the fence, and that I was most likely to find him within call. Mother has allowed him to make a gate of communication between his shrubbery and ours, not many paces from the arbour where I first discovered that I adored him. I found him this morning standing close by this gate, with a very grave countenance, evidently on the watch for me, and I saw at a glance that he had read all about the murder.

He had, and we talked the hideous story over together.

"How will it affect Mr. Arden?" I asked.

"If he is the guilty wretch you think him it may affect him most terribly. The man Morel has been taken red-handed, and cannot escape condemnation. If he is the murderer of Denmark Street; if your step-father prompted that murder, as you believe, he may, out of sheer devilry, make a full confession before he goes to the guillotine, denounce his accomplice, and die in the odour of sanctity."

"And then my mother will know everything, and the rest of her life will be made miserable," said I.

My step-father left us this evening. I felt sick with apprehension when I saw mother bidding him good-bye in the hall, while the carriage waited to drive him to the station; she so full of kindliness and concern for his comfort on the cold night-journey, he pale and sombre, speaking with evident effort.

"You are looking so ill to-night, Ambrose," she said. "I fear you are hardly equal to the journey, and the trouble that may come afterwards."

"I must face both, Clara. My chief anxiety is about you and your peace of mind," he answered gravely. "If you will only be true to yourself, I fear nothing. You have your daughter and her husband to think of; new duties, new ties, the beginning of a new existence."

It seemed to me as if he were renouncing all share in her life, all claim to her affection. He looked at me earnestly, questioningly, and then, as I made no movement towards him, he said quietly—

"Good night and good-bye, Daisy."

He turned on the threshold and took my mother in his arms and kissed her forehead and her lips with a sudden fervour that transformed him.

The pallid, careworn face flushed and smiled, the dull and sunken eyes brightened. It was for a moment only. His valet warned him that there was no time to lose, he stepped into the brougham, the door was shut, and he was gone.

CHAPTER XII.

DAISY'S DIARY.

IT is the eve of my wedding day, the eve of St. Valentine's Day; Gilbert is to be my Valentine to-morrow and for ever.

And now in this deep silence of after midnight I will close the record of my life as an unmarried woman. The life that will begin to-morrow will mark the opening of a new volume in my history, but the old book shall be my friend and confidant still, for I shall be able to praise my husband in these pages as I should never dare to praise him to any living listener, least of all to his modest, unpretending self.

I shall close the record of my girlish years, and with it, I hope, closes the tragedy of my own and my mother's life. God grant that bloodshed and guilt and treachery may have no further influence upon her life and mine, and that the road that lies before us may pass through a peaceful and a smiling land, where crime and sin will have no part in our destiny.

The interval between my step-father's journey to Paris and the end of the year was a time of keenest anxiety for me, and for Gilbert, who shared and lightened all my cares. We watched the three principal Paris papers, which Gilbert ordered to be sent him daily, and watched with intense expectation for any notice of the murderer Morel. The actual facts recorded were few, beyond those particulars of the murder which had appeared in the first instance; but there was a great deal of descriptive writing bearing more or less upon the crime. Something of this kind appeared in one or other of the papers nearly every day. Sometimes there was a paragraph about the prisoner's antecedents, the part he took in the riots and brutalities of the Commune, the manner of his escape when the Versailles troops got possession of Paris, and many other facts or fictions about his past life.

Gilbert told me that I must not believe more than one-fourth of any such article or paragraphs in a Parisian newspaper.

One day there appeared a long account of the villa which was the scene of the murder, an article in which the luxury and splendour of the house were minutely described. Another article in the same paper gave a glowing description of the prisoner's cousin, a beautiful young woman, married to one of the richest men in Paris. Scandal about this young woman and her mother was freely published, cruel imputations against their character; but there was not one line in any of the papers which hinted at Claude Morel's identity with the murderer of Denmark Street.

"The police know all about him," said Gilbert, "but they are keeping dark. A man cannot be tried for two crimes at the same time. Were Morel acquitted he could be arrested and brought to London to be confronted with the witnesses—the landlady and the tailor's journeyman—who could identify the murderer of

Denmark Street; but I do not see the remotest chance of his acquittal."

My step-father remained in Paris for nearly a month, during which time he wrote at least twice a week to my mother. She read portions of his letters to me. He had seen the police, and they had told him that there was very little doubt of the prisoner's execution. The crime was too utterly brutal to enlist the sympathies of even a French jury. He would be found guilty without extenuating circumstances. He would perhaps appeal to the Court of Cassation, but his appeal would be rejected.

In a later letter my step-father wrote that he had with great difficulty obtained an interview with the prisoner. He had taxed him with the murder in Denmark Street, but Morel had denied all knowledge of that crime. The letter described him as an obdurate villain.

The trial took place in the second week of December. The prisoner's cousin, Madame Perez, was the chief witness against him. She described how he had appealed to her for money, or for jewels to convert into money, two hours before the murder; and how she had refused to give him either money or jewels, upon which he left the house, angry and menacing. She described how she was startled from her sleep by the sound of footsteps in her room, and on opening her eyes saw the prisoner standing before her toilet-table, deliberately filling his pockets with her jewels, which she had worn in great profusion upon that particular evening. She told the court how she had sprung from her bed, intending to ring for help, but before she could reach the electric-bell the accused struck her to the ground. She remembered nothing after that blow, which had inflicted a permanent injury upon the sight of one eye. She had only just recovered from a nervous fever which had followed upon her return to consciousness.

The appearance of this witness in the court excited a profound interest, said the papers. She is described as a very beautiful woman. Her evidence was given in some parts reluctantly, at other times with a rush of indignant feeling. When asked by the prisoner if she had not been his mistress, she passionately repelled the accusation. She admitted that she had once loved him, but that was before she knew the worthlessness of his character. She spoke in the highest terms of the murdered Louise. She denied any knowledge of the fact that the brother and sister had adopted names which were not their own. She had never heard the name of Morel in association with either of them.

The evidence of the gendarme who arrested the murderer red-handed was conclusive. The blood of his victim and the jewels which he had stolen were found upon him. There was little need of deliberation. The verdict was guilty, without extenuating circumstances. The sentence was death.

I can never forget my mother's face when Gilbert told her the doom of Claude Morel. We went together to the morning-room where she was sitting at work, her great basket of flannel and calico on the hearthrug in front of her chair, her pale, anxious face intent upon her stitching. In all this time of suspense she had employed herself chiefly in visiting the poor and working for them. She told me that it was only by constant occupation, useful and mechanical work, that she could steady her nerves, and prevent herself from dwelling incessantly upon the tragedy of her life.

She listened quietly while Gilbert read the verdict and the sentence, and then, with bent head and clasped hands, she murmured those awful words which she had spoken to her husband when she first read of Morel's crime—

"'Vengeance is mine. I will repay, saith the Lord.'"

How often and how often in the time past she must have repeated that terrible text!

She received a letter from her husband the same evening, but it could tell her nothing which the paper had not told her already, except that he intended to remain in Paris for a few days to see if there were any likelihood of a commutation of the sentence.

Five days afterwards my step-father walked into the drawing-room at nine o'clock in the evening, unannounced and unexpected. He had come from Paris by the morning mail.

"I waited till the eve of the execution, Clara," he said, when my mother had welcomed him.

Gilbert and I were sitting at chess in a nook near the fire-place. We stood up to greet him, but kept aloof, as if he had been a stranger.

"It is decided then. There will be no reprieve," said my mother.

"None."

"Then there will be at least one villain less in the world," said I.

He looked at me. Never to my dying day can I forget the agonized reproachfulness of that look. It was a look that made me feel as if I were the ingrate and the traitor, and he only the injured. I saw the picture of my happy child-hood—as they say a drowning man sees all his past life in the moment before death. I saw myself with my arms round that man's neck and my cheek against his breast; saw myself soothed

and watched over in hours of childish illness;
taught and counselled, and amused and trained
by that keen intellect; loved and petted, with
an inexhaustible patience and an unvarying
tenderness, by that grave student, for whom all
the world of thought was an open book.

How often, how continually, day after day, had
he laid aside his dearest occupation to devote
himself to the education and the amusement of
a child! Yes, he had done all this; he had
sacrificed his inclinations, he had made himself
a slave for my mother's sake, and to win her he
had plotted my father's death.

My eyelids fell and my heart beat fast beneath
that mute reproach; but for me his crime was
an unpardonable crime. I dared not pity him,
even in his agony of remorse; for such pity
would have been treachery to my dead father.

My mother urged him to take some refresh-
ment after his journey, and gave her orders to
the butler to that end, but he declared that he
had dined in London.

"You must have had some time in town

between the arrival of the Paris train and the departure of the 7.50 from Paddington?" said my mother.

"Yes; I had nearly two hours; time enough to dine, and to transact a little business in the city."

"In the city? But all the offices would be closed at that time?"

"Not the office I wanted."

He was looking very ill, and had grown thinner in the few weeks of absence. I saw my mother observing him anxiously, as he sat in front of the fire, warming his wasted hands before the burning logs. He talked with some show of cheerfulness, asked about the preparations for the marriage, and for Christmas. Was it to be a gay Christmas at River Lawn?

"Gay!" echoed mother; "how could I think of gaiety at such a time? My thoughts have been fixed upon one subject. Every effort of my mind has been not to think too perpetually of the man who is to die to-morrow."

"Of the man who is to die to-morrow," he

repeated solemnly. "Death cancels all wrong-doing—at least the Law thinks so. The worst *that* you can do to a murderer is to kill him."

He rose slowly, and moved about the room in his old restless way, and then came over to my mother, and bent over her and kissed her.

"Don't sit up for me, Clara," he said; "I have letters to write, proofs to look over, the accumulations of a month. I have sent Ames over to the cottage with my despatch-box. I shall sit there very late, most likely."

"Not to-night, Ambrose, surely not to-night! There will be plenty of time to-morrow," remonstrated mother.

"No, I have left everything to the last. There will be no time to-morrow. Good night, dear love."

He nodded to Gilbert and me, a cool, curt nod, and was gone before my mother could remonstrate further.

"How pale and haggard he looks!" she said. "I was wrong to let him go to Paris upon such a painful business, in his weak health. What would Sir Andrew say to me if he knew how his advice had been disregarded?"

"Sir Andrew recommended rest, I suppose," said Gilbert.

"He told my husband that it was essential for him to take life quietly."

"Ah, doctors tell us that—but will the heart and brain cease from troubling, at a physician's bidding?"

My mother sighed, and sank into melancholy silence; and our game went on slowly, quietly, in the silent room, where there was no sound but the light fall of wood ashes on the hearth.

My mother came to me at seven o'clock next morning, and told me that her husband had been at work all night. She had watched his lamp from her bedroom window, being herself too agitated to sleep, or even to lie down for more than half an hour at a time. The lamp had been burning till daybreak, when she saw it extinguished.

I too had watched that lamp, wondering what

the guilty soul was suffering in that long night—
whether he wished himself in the condemned
cell where that vulgar villain was waiting the
dawn of his last day, whether he would have
welcomed the knife as a short, sharp cure for the
pangs of a guilty conscience.

My step-father had never before spent a whole
night at the cottage, and indeed had seldom
occupied himself in his library of an evening.
This unaccustomed night-watch made my mother
uneasy, and she asked me to go across the road
with her, to see if there were anything amiss.

"He may have fallen asleep at his desk," she
said, "and in a cold room; for I dare say he has
not been careful to keep the fire burning all
night."

He had dismissed his valet when he went over
to the cottage, and was alone there, except for
the existence of an elderly woman who lived in
the back premises, cleaned and aired the rooms,
and made fires. We went across the road together, mother and I, in the bleak winter morning. The sky was red above the leafless elm-

tops, towards London, but gray and gloomy in every other direction. The neglected garden, and the cottage itself, looked very dull and dreary in the chilly dawn, the sodden creepers hanging from the walls, the plaster blotted with damp.

"What a dismal house! To think that Ambrose and his son lived in it for ever so many years," murmured my mother.

She had only to turn the handle of the door to go in—there was no bolt or lock to shut us out. I followed her into the dark passage, and into the room on the right of the porch, the room which my step-father called his den, a room lined with books from floor to ceiling.

"Yes," whispered my mother, "he has fallen asleep."

The atmosphere was close and hot, and reeked with the odour of lamp oil. A pair of candles had burnt down to the sockets, and the ashes were gray in the grate.

My step-father's head had fallen upon his folded arms, and upon the table in front of him

there was a long official envelope, directed in a
large firm hand—" For my wife."

I read the words across my mother's shoulder
as she bent down to speak to her husband, and I
guessed what dreadful thing had happened, and
what new horror she would have to bear.

"Come away, mother, come away!" I cried;
"he is dead! I know he is dead!"

She bent over him still, and lifted the heavy
head, and looked at the ashen countenance. Yes,
it was the end. Death cancels every wrong.
Ambrose Arden's words of the night before came
back to me as we stood there in that awful
silence which his voice could never break again.

Vain now all hope of keeping the truth from
my mother. That envelope, no doubt, contained
the admission of his guilt. She would know, and
she would suffer from that knowledge.

She burst into tears as she hung over the lifeless clay.

"Oh, Daisy," she sobbed, "he has gone from
us for ever. Our voices cannot reach him now.
I was never half grateful enough for his love or
his goodness to me."

"Don't lament him, mother—he was not worthy," I said; but my tears were streaming too; and I saw the dead man as he seemed to me in my childhood, before my father's death, before he had begun to plot murder.

We knew before that day was ended that he had died from an overdose of chloral. He had had strength of will and purpose to throw the empty bottle under the grate, where it was found broken among the cinders. Thus it was that mother and I did not suspect a suicide, when we found him cold and lifeless at his desk. .

She has not told me the contents of the packet, but I know from her manner that she has nothing more to learn about my father's death, albeit Claude Morel died without having made any admission of his guilt. She has been full of sadness since her husband's funeral, in spite of her brave attempt to sympathize with Gilbert and me. The wedding has been delayed for nearly two months in deference to my step-father's memory and the *bienséances*. The coroner's inquest resulted in a verdict of "Death by misadventure."

CHAPTER XIII.

AMBROSE ARDEN'S CONFESSION.

TO-MORROW morning, before the day is old, Claude Morel will expiate his last and worst crime on the scaffold. He is now sitting in his condemned cell writing his confession, the story of the murder in Denmark Street, the hideous history of his crime and of mine, which he has sworn that he will leave behind him to-morrow morning to be published broadcast to all civilized Europe before to-morrow night.

This room, where I sit in the deep of night, in a silence rarely broken by some belated footfall in the lane; this room, lined round with books, mute companions of my joyless manhood, is *my* condemned cell. The day that will dawn in a few hours will be as surely my day of doom, as it will be Claude Morel's. The sentence

of death that was pronounced upon him was a
sentence of death pronounced upon me.   His fate
involved my fate.   When I made him the instru-
ment of my crime I made myself his slave.

Oh, my beloved, the only idol of my life, it
is for you I write the history of my sin.   No
other eye but yours need ever look upon these
lines, unless you so will it; and I do not think
you will expose this dark record of weak passion
and unscrupulous crime to an indifferent public.
Let the world know my story only as it will be
told by my accomplice—a ghastly story, cruelly
and brutally told, no doubt.   These details of
my temptation and my fall are for you alone ;
for you who may perhaps execrate my memory
just a little less if I urge my one plea for mercy
—I loved you with a love that was stronger than
honour or manhood—stronger than all the in-
stincts of a life that had been blameless whilst it
was passionless—a love that made me a villain.

I first saw Claude Morel at an Italian public-
house in Greek Street, where I went to distribute
some money, collected from a few of my friends,

among the distressed Communists who had come
to London for a refuge, and who were some of
them almost starving. Most of the people
assembled in that upstairs room over the tavern
bar were depressed and dispirited by their
necessities, and had very little to say, except to
express their thankfulness for the aid which I
took them; but Morel had a great deal to say
about the political situation in France. He
spoke well, and I was interested in his fervid
eloquence, and in the latent passion which
burned in every phrase. I put him down as a
dangerous man in any country, a firebrand in
such a city as Paris.

He heard, *en passant*, that the friend who had
given more than half the sum I had collected
was Robert Hattrell. I saw the startling effect
of that name upon him, and I was hardly
surprised when he followed me into the street
and began to question me about my friend. I
was surprised, however, at the malignity of his
speech, and the intensity of malice which
betrayed itself in his tone and manner.

He told me the story of a sister's wrongs. She had been fooled and duped by a wealthy Englishman, who coolly refused any reparation for the wrong he had done—for a girl's blighted name and broken heart. He was not very explicit in his charges, but this was the kind of thing which he gave me to understand, and he was just as vindictive as if he had been certain of his facts.

I heard the true story of the case from your husband afterwards, and he gave me his honour that his worst offence had been a sentimental flirtation with a grisette, an innocent unsophisticated girl, with whom he had been almost seriously in love. His attachment had just stopped short of a serious passion; and he had but just escaped the folly of a low marriage.

I believed my friend's statement, and thought no more of Morel's malignity, which I did not suppose would ever take any overt form, though I considered it my duty to warn Robert Hatrell of the existence of this vindictive feeling, and to let him know that his enemy was in London.

He laughed at the man's threats, and the subject was dismissed by us both.

I had almost forgotten it when I met Morel in Gower Street one afternoon on my way from the Museum to the Metropolitan Railway Station. He told me his troubles, the difficulty of getting employment, his schemes and inventions, which sounded chimerical in the last degree, and his want of money. He talked again of my friend Hatrell, but I stopped him peremptorily.

"I have heard your sister's story from my friend's own lips," I said; "and I am convinced that your version is a tissue of lies."

He was furious at this. He upbraided me for believing a gentleman in preference to a man of the people. It was the old story. The well-born seducer could always escape the consequences of his wrong-doing; but for once in a way the world should see that retribution may follow wrong. Robert Hatrell had broken his sister's heart, and had grossly insulted her; and he meant to be even with him.

He asked me for half a sovereign, but I had

only a few shillings about me; so he gave me a card with a written address upon it, begging me to send him a post-office order next day.

I have since discovered that he had appealed to your husband for money, and had been sternly refused; and no doubt that refusal was a more unpardonable offence than any sin against his sister.

It was within a week of this accidental encounter with Morel that I received an unexpected visit from my father's old lawyer. He came to Lamford in order with his own lips to communicate some very wonderful news. A second cousin of my father's had lately died in Chicago, leaving me his residuary legatee, and, with some insignificant exceptions, the inheritor of a large fortune acquired in trade. I had never even heard of Matthew Arden, who had begun life with a small estate in the East Riding, where he farmed his own land, and had ended life as one of the richest merchants in Chicago. For me this fortune was a fortune dropped from the clouds.

I was astounded, but hardly elated by this sudden change from poverty to wealth. The studious life I was leading was the only life I should ever care to lead. Money, except so far as the indulgence of my taste as a collector of books, could be of very little use to me; and even my taste in books was inexpensive. I did not pine for tall copies or rare editions. All I valued in a book was its contents. At this time I had not attained to the fine instinct of a collector.

I told my old friend that I should make no difference in my mode of life, and that I should tell my son nothing of this change in our fortunes for some time to come. I begged the good old family lawyer to exercise the discretion which had always been his distinguishing quality, and to take care that no newspaper paragraphs descriptive of my unexpected luck had their source in his office.

When the lawyer left me I sat alone among my books, and thought over the change in my fortunes. A stroke of luck which would have

made most men half mad with joy left me cold.
What could wealth give me? Nothing, for it
could not give me you.

Yes, Clara, it was of you, and you only, that I
thought, as I tried to estimate the value of these
riches that had fallen into my lap. What was
their worth to me; what could they do for me;
what could they buy for me? Nothing, nothing,
nothing!

I was still a young man; I was not ill-looking;
and I had some pretensions to intellectual
power. Hitherto poverty had exercised its
restraining influence upon me. I had lived
obscurely, remote from the world. I might now,
if I pleased, make a figure in society, live in
a fine house, and surround myself with fine
people.

I had no more inclination to do this than I had
to head an expedition to the North Pole. Society
had no pleasure to offer me. Neither house nor
garden nor stable had any attraction for me. I
was not a sportsman. I was not a yachtsman.
I had never felt the faintest interest in a race on

land or water. I had but one passion, one dream, one desire upon earth, or beyond the earth—and that was you. My whole being resolved itself into one ardent longing—to win you.

I loved you from the first day I saw you. Oh, God! how vividly I can recall that first day and hour, that casual meeting which decided the whole course of my life, for good or evil! Your face flashes out of the shadowy distance beyond the lamplight—a vision of gladness and beauty —as it shone upon me that clear October morning, when you stood before me leaning against your husband's arm, newly returned from your honeymoon, a two-months bride.

You remember our first meeting, Clara; how I looked in through the open gate and saw you standing deep in conversation with your husband and his architect, who was holding an open plan for you both to look at. I had made Mr. Hatrell's acquaintance a few days before, when he came down to Lamford alone, and we happened to travel in the same railway carriage.

He introduced himself to me as my future

neighbour, and insisted upon giving me a lift in his fly from the station, though I told him it was my habit to walk home.

"I want you to tell me all about the neighbourhood," he said.

This had broken the ice, and on this second time of seeing each other we exchanged friendly salutations through the open gate; and then as I lingered a little he called me into the garden and introduced me to his wife.

I remember your courteous greeting—so courteous yet so careless. How could you dream that I was to be so potent a factor in your sum of life! How could you guess that the lovely face which you turned towards me, so unconscious of its power, was to change the whole current of my existence—to make me first your passionate lover, and next your husband's murderer!

Yes, Clara, his murderer. From that hour I was foredoomed to do evil for your sake. I was fated to blight your happiness, and to miss being happy, even though I gained the wages of my crime.

What did I think of you that day? Only that
you were the most enchanting woman I had ever
seen, and that Robert Hatrell was a man for all
other men to envy. My thoughts went no further
than that on the first day. I thought of your
loveliness as I should have thought of some rare
flower—the white chalice of the Victoria regia
floating in the faint tropical haze of a still water-
pool, the pale purple or vivid gold of some fairy-
like orchid—something delicately beautiful that
did not come within the scope of my life. I had
no more definite thought of you than that; yet
afterwards I knew that I had loved you from the
first. The change was in myself, not in my
thoughts. A slow consuming fever was kindled
in me that day which has never ceased to burn.
Little by little, by infinitesimal stages, it has
burnt up heart and brain.

Your husband liked me, and you were always
kind. For the first years of our acquaintance we
met but rarely; and it was not till you were
established at River Lawn that I came to be
intimately acquainted with you both, and gradu-

ally to be almost one of the family.   Daisy was
the link which united us.   I had the good fortune
to win the child's love, and this assured me of
the mother's friendship.   You loved books, while
your husband cared little for reading or any
intellectual pursuit, being, above all, a man of
action.   I was able thus to supply something
wanting in your life, and to fill a place which he
ought to have been able to fill.   I was the
adviser of your studies, and the sharer of your
ideas.   I felt sometimes as if I were the husband
of your intellect, as he was the husband of your
heart.

Had I ever seen any wavering in your fidelity
to him, any weariness of the tie that bound you
to him, I do not believe that I should have tried
to turn it to my own advantage.   I could not
have degraded you by one unworthy prayer.   I
could not couple dishonour with your image.

There were times when our calm friendship,
our mutual love for your child, which kept us in
touch with one another, seemed to me almost
enough for my happiness.   I felt as if I could

have gone on contentedly thus, to old age, making a quiet third in your life—now with your husband, now with your daughter, always subordinate— the shadow beside your sunshine. And then, while I was cheating myself with these calm thoughts, a wave of passion would sweep over my being; a demon of jealousy would rend and tear me; and I could not endure to be with you in the serene atmosphere of domestic love. Your husband's every look and every tone tortured me.

You have both of you reproached me sometimes for keeping aloof, for burying myself among my books, and shunning the hospitalities of River Lawn. If you could have seen me in those sup- posed-studious intervals, you would have seen a man possessed of devils, given over to perdition.

Imagine these years of alternate storm and calm; imagine a mind and heart burnt up by one devouring passion, worn out with the monotony of despair; and then think what my thoughts must have been as I sat in my solitude and brooded over the worthlessness of my newly- acquired wealth.

Had you been free, fortune would have meant everything for me. Had you been free—the widow of a rich man—it would have been a hard thing to approach you as a pauper. My pride would have revolted against owing all to you, fortune as well as happiness. But now—now that I was rich—your equal at least in fortune, my motives could not inspire doubt even in the meanest mind. Were I to wed you no malicious worldling could ever say of me, "He gained all by that lucky marriage."

Were you but free!

I began to meditate upon the uncertainty of life, and to picture to myself the accidents and sudden unforeseen diseases by which men as young and vigorous as Robert Hatrell are sometimes taken away. I thought of railway accidents, and imagination conjured up the picture of some such catastrophe in all its vivid detail—an engine off the line, a coach or two wrecked, and Robert Hatrell lying dead upon the side of the embankment. I pictured the sudden horror of his homecoming upon the shrouded bier. Your agony, your tears. I passed over those lightly, thinking of how it would be my lot to console you, slowly, patiently to win you back to happiness and a new love. I never doubted your love for him ; I knew that your heart was entirely his; but I thought I had an influence over your mind which would speedily ripen into love, he being removed.

I understood you so little, you see, Clara. I had not fathomed the mystery of your heart. He has been dead nine years, and you love him still. You have never loved me.

I thought of the river, saw him rowing towards the sunset, with his strong, slow stroke, in such a scene as our English landscape-painters love ; the village church beyond the low line of rushes; the clustering willows, pale in the evening haze ; the glory of the sunset behind church-tower and tall elms.

I thought that even on that placid river there were possibilities of danger—a boat of silly, chattering Cockneys upset, a strong man swimming to their rescue, and losing his life in the struggle to save those unknown lives. Such things have been.

I thought of fevers which seize men suddenly in the full vigour of youth. I thought of insidious diseases which creep upon a man unsuspected, and sap the citadel before he knows that Death in one of his numerous disguises is at the door.

Last of all, I thought of Morel, and his threats of vengeance.

I laughed at the notion. Harmless thunder, no doubt. It is common enough for angry men to threaten; but threatened men live.

There was something in my recollection of Claude Morel which made me dwell upon his image in that long reverie, as the lovely light of the June afternoon slowly faded, and the gold of the western sky shone into my room, dazzling my dreaming eyes. I recall the colour of the sunset, the feeling of the air as it gradually cooled into evening. I recall every half-unconscious impression of hours which marked the crisis of my life, and saw me change from an honest man to a villain.

There were in Morel's tone and manner certain indications of a malignity which I had never seen in any other man. There was a concentration of purpose, a resolute intention to injure, which must ultimately take some definite form, I told myself, unless cowardice should intervene. And I did not think Morel a coward. The man had so little to lose. His fortunes were desperate enough to make him daring.

What if the opportunity arose, and he were to murder the man he hated—the man who had refused to help him in his distress? I implicitly believed Robert Hatrell's account of his love affair, and I did not give Morel credit for caring much about his sister's reputation. He had tried to make money out of the Englishman's caprice, but he had failed ignominiously. Hence, and hence only, that rancorous hatred. He was of the temper which in the hour of misfortune would turn like a tiger against the fortunate — the temper of men who surge up out of the paving-stones and gutters of every great city in the time of revolution, and who do evil for evil's sake. Upon the conscience of such a man as that murder would sit lightly.

What if he really meant murder? I pictured that sinister figure lurking in the rustic lanes, lying hidden in a dry flowery ditch, under the spreading hedgerow, ready with pistol or knife when his enemy passsd by.

Opportunity? Why, if he meant murder, it would be easy enough for him to create his opportunity. But when the thing was done, when that gnawing rage had satiated itself, there would be nothing gained but the gratification of his anger, and there would be the hazard of the gallows.

The murderer's craft may minimize that risk. The old saw, that murder will out, has proved a lying proverb of late years. The art of murder has progressed with the march of civilization, and the modern murderer is more than a match for the modern policeman.

I recalled a murder which had interested me curiously years before, when I read the account of it in a London newspaper, I being then remote from London, amid the stillness of the Welsh hills.

It happened in the days when trade union was called conspiracy, and when the law of the land bore heavily upon workmen who banded themselves together against their employer. A certain set of men had conspired; there had been outrages and violence in a certain northern city, and attempted arson. The ringleaders were denounced by one of themselves, were tried, found guilty, and sentenced to transportation for life. The man who betrayed them dared not remain in his native city. *There* he knew himself to be a marked man; but he thought he would be safe in London, under an assumed name.

He came to London, got employment readily, for he was a clever workman, and funded the price of his treachery as a nest-egg for his old age.

Going homewards one day, at his dinner hour, he walked along a quiet street in Soho, which he was in the habit of passing through daily. Midway this street is intersected by a narrow alley. As the man came in front of the opening he was shot dead by some one standing in the alley, waiting for him to pass. No one ever knew what

hand fired the shot.   It was in broad daylight,
in the heart of a busy district, but the murderer
disappeared as easily as if he had been spirit and
not flesh.   I tell you of this long-forgotten crime,
Clara, because it was the nucleus of evil thoughts
which slowly took the form of murder.

My wicked scheme did not shape itself all at
once.   For many days and nights I was haunted
by the image of Claude Morel, haunted by the
tones of his voice, the lurid light in his eyes when
he talked of his enemy.   Again and again I
found myself mentally measuring the force of
that hatred which had expressed itself in biting
tones and malevolent looks.   Did it amount to so
much, or so much, or so much?   Was it really
strong enough to plan and accomplish an assas-
sination, in broad daylight, in the streets of
London, a deed as daring as the murder of the
workman who betrayed his comrades?

All this time my life went on upon the old
lines—the calm monotony of rustic surroundings,
the unvarying graciousness of your friendship.
Your child sat beside me at her books, under the

willow, or hung upon my shoulder in her exube-
rance of love; and there was no instinct in her
childish mind to warn her that the man she loved
and trusted had given himself over to the powers
of hell.

I am not sufficiently orthodox to believe in a
Personal Devil any more than I believe in a
Personal God; yet in those days I could not
divest myself of the feeling that wicked influences outside my own existence had got hold
of me—that the hideous hopes and schemes that
I was for ever revolving in my mind were
prompted by a power of iniquity greater than my
own.

While the wicked web was slowly spreading,
the man who was the incarnation of my own
sinful longing appeared upon the scene. He had
written me two or three begging letters after that
chance meeting in Gower Street, and I had sent
him small sums of money, such amounts as a
man of my supposed means might send to such
an applicant. These concessions had made him
bolder, and he came to my house in the dusk of

a summer evening, having walked all the way
from Staines. He had just the railway fare to
Staines, he told me, and no more. I took him in
and fed him, and let him sit at my table and
vapour about his inchoate inventions, all burked
for the want of capital. I let him talk of your
husband, and I answered all his questions about
the man he hated. I told him of Robert
Hatrell's happy and peaceful life, his prosperity,
his last fancy for sinking four thousand pounds
in the purchase of a few acres of land to increase
his pleasure grounds.

"In your native South, I take it, you would be
able to buy an olive wood and a vineyard with
that money?" I said.

He nodded yes, and went on eating and drinking, in a meditative silence.

"Now, were any man as savage a foe to Robert
Hatrell as you pretend to be," I said, after a long
pause, "he would have a good chance of taking
his revenge and making his fortune some time
next week."

He looked at me wonderingly, and I explained

that Hatrell would have to pay for the land in
Bank of England notes. It was an old-fashioned
etiquette with solicitors to expect to be paid in
bank-notes, even when a man's cheque was as
good as the bank paper. Hatrell would go up
to London on an appointed day, cash his
cheque at his bank, and then carry the money
to the solicitor's office. I told him casually
the name and address of the bank, and the
name and address of the solicitor; and I saw
him sitting there before me, with his eyes kind-
ling like two burning coals, and his under-lip
trembling curiously as his halting breath came
and went.

"Hatrell and his money will be safe enough,"
he muttered at last. "A man can't be robbed
and murdered in broad daylight in such a city as
London."

"There you show your foreign ignorance of
our manners and customs," I said; and then I
gave him the brief history of several metropolitan assassinations which had occurred within
my memory.

He became very serious and silent, sitting before his empty plate, with his chin drooping on his chest, his inky brows bent in a thoughtful frown. Suddenly, after an interval which seemed long, he lifted his head and turned and looked at me, with a devilish cunning in his eyes.

"You hate Robert Hatrell as much as I do," he said. "You are in love with his wife, I dare say."

"Nonsense. I am only trying to prove to you that all your talk about hatred and revenge is so much melodramatic bluster, and that you haven't the slighest intention of injuring my friend."

"Your friend! your friend!" he repeated, mockingly.

And then, after another interval of silence, during which he walked over to the window and stood looking across the placid summer twilight, in the direction of River Lawn, he came over to me and stood in front of me, looking at me fixedly and emphasizing every sentence with a sharp rap of his knuckles upon the table.

"You want that man killed, so do I; *cela se comprend.* I would kill him for sixpence; kill him for the mere pleasure of making him understand that he was a fool to trifle with Claude Morel's sister, and a greater fool to insult Claude Morel. I take too lofty a view of the situation perhaps. That is in my blood. We Provençals do not easily pardon an injury or an insult. I would kill him for sixpence; but I would much rather kill him for four thousand pounds. You say the purchase is to be completed next week?"

I nodded yes. My dry lips refused to speak.

"Let me know the day and hour. Let me know, if you can, the route he is likely to take from Pall Mall to Lincoln's-Inn-Fields. Give me twenty pounds to be ready for what I have to do, and in order that I may have a few pounds about me to get me out of England in case of failure. Do this, and you may lie down to-night secure in the thought that Robert Hatrell's days are numbered, and that his wife will soon be his widow."

I gave him two ten-pound notes without a word.

"I'll think about the other part of the business," I told him.

"Remember, if I am to act you will have to be prompt and decisive," he said. "I can't stir a step without exact details. I shall shift my lodgings to-morrow, so as to be near the scene of action. My present quarters at Camden Town are too far afield."

His devilish coolness was too much for me. I told him I had been talking at random. I meant nothing except to test him. He had proved himself a greater villain than I had thought possible, and I never wanted to see his face again.

"You will think better of that," he said. "I'll telegraph my address to-morrow morning, and I shall wait for your instructions."

Not till the last moment—not till I crossed the threshold of the Post Office at Reading an hour after your husband left for London on that fatal day—did I make up my mind that I was going to do this hideous thing. Again and again

and again with agonizing iteration I had argued
the question. I had told myself that this
horror could not be; that I, Ambrose Arden, was
not the stuff of which murderers are made; and
again and again and yet again my thoughts had
gone back to the pit of hell, and I had pictured
you free to return my love, and I had thought
that such love must finally win its reward;
that in all intense passion there is a magnetic
power which can compel responsive passion, as
fire will spread from one burning fabric to
another that was dark and cold till the flame
touched it.

When your husband left the gate that morning
I knew that I must act at once, or never. I
walked to the station, caught the slow train that
left half an hour after the express by which he
travelled, and went to Reading, where the word-
ing of my telegram was not likely to arouse
official curiosity. I had only one fact to communicate—the hour of Hatrell's appointment with
Florestan's solicitor. Morel knew the locality of
the Bank, and it would be for him to watch and

find out the route taken from Cockspur Street to Lincoln's Inn.

Can you think what my feelings were that night when you came over to this house at ten o'clock to tell me that your husband had not returned?

I knew then that one of the most hellish schemes ever hatched had been carried out to the bitter end, and that the murder had been done. Did Judas feel as I did, I wonder, before he went and hanged himself? I did not give myself up to that blind despair of remorse which moved him who betrayed his Master. I was baser, harder, viler than Judas—for I stood that night with your hands clasped in mine, pretending to comfort you, repeating lying assurances that all would be well, while my heart beat madly with the thought that you were free, and that it would be my life's dear labour to win your love.

And through those days of doubt and horror I acted my part, and hypocrisy came easy to me.

Anything was easy, so long as I was with you, consoling, advising, sustaining; you leaning upon me in your innocent unconsciousness of the deep flood of passion that surged below the steadfast quietude which I had schooled myself to maintain.

Throughout those days I was haunted by the fear that the murderer would be caught, tried, and condemned, and that he would reveal my part in his crime. I feared that which has now come to pass, after a respite of nearly nine years.

Then came the darkest period of all my hateful life—the period of your illness, when your life hung in the balance, when every day that dawned might be your last on earth. I lived through that time, a time of fear and trembling, which I shuddered even to remember, years afterwards.

And then, and then came my great reward— the reward of treachery and bloodshed, base betrayal of a noble friend, a long tissue of lies and hypocrisies; then, after years of patience,

during which I had shrunk with an uncon-
querable hesitancy from putting my fate to the
touch, I had the price of my sin. Your love,
no! That love for which I had sinned was no
nearer my winning after seven years' apprentice-
ship than it was while my victim lived. You
gave me gratitude—gratitude to me who had
blighted your happy life. You rewarded me for
the steadfastness of a friendship which in somewise linked my image with that of your murdered
husband. Oh, how you will abhor my memory
when you look back upon your self-sacrifice,
your generous payment of a fancied debt! How
you will hate yourself for having been trapped
into a loveless union with the man who plotted
your husband's death, who was to all intents and
purposes his murderer!

Well, it is all over now. I grasped the Dead
Sea fruit, and tasted the bitterness of its ashen
core. I knew that you did not love me—and I
was more miserable as your husband than when I
waited at your gate as a suitor. There were
glimpses of Paradise then—gleams of hope

shining on my crime-darkened spirit; but afterwards, when I had constrained you to be mine—
when I had won all that Fate could give me, I
knew that your heart was with the dead.

> " Nought's had, all's spent,
>   When our desire is got without content."

That was the motto of my life.

Then came a new horror—a haunting fear of
the dead, which I take to have been rather
physical than mental. Could I, disciple of
Schopenhauer and Hartmann,—I who had
graduated in the school of exact science, and
reduced every thought and feeling to its logical
sequence, admitting nothing which my mind
could not conceive—could I be the sport of
ghostly forms and unreal voices? I to be
haunted and paralysed by the dread of a shadow
—I to tremble and turn cold on entering your
husband's study, lest I should see a pale image
of the dead seated where the living man used to
sit—I to walk those familiar gardens with an
ever-present dread of a well-known footstep
sounding behind me, or, when no imaginary

sound pursued me, with an absolute certainty
that I was being followed by the noiseless movements of a phantom! I to become the slave
of such fears—I who believe in nothing beyond
the limitations of our understanding—who have
restricted all my speculations to the real and the
finite!

I knew from the first that these horrors had
their source in shattered nerves and broken health.
I knew that I was as much a sufferer from
physical causes as the victim of alcoholic poisoning who sees devils and vermin about his bed.
Yet the thing was as real to me as if I had been
the firmest believer in supernatural influences;
and I suffered as much from these false appear-
ances and imaginary sounds as the believer could
have suffered. *That* is one form which retribution
has taken. The other form has been my ever-
present sense of disappointment in not having won
your heart. Tortured thus, life has been only a
synonym for suffering; and I can look forward
coldly and calmly to the coming daylight, when
I shall have ceased to live.

How can I plead to you at the close of this full and deliberate confession? How dare I hope that you can have any feeling except loathing for the writer of these lines? For myself, therefore, I will ask nothing. I ask only that you will be kind to my son, who, if Morel carries out his threat, must bear henceforward the burden of a name blurred by his father's infamy. He has a fine character, and will reward your kindness. His mother was one of the best and purest of women; think of him as inheriting her virtues and not my dark and evil spirit. It is not in his nature either to love as I have loved, or to sin as I have sinned.

Yes, you will be good to my son, I know, Clara. You will forget that there is one drop of my Judas blood in his veins. You may know now, in this day of confessions, why he left us—why he broke the tie between him and Daisy, and shook the dust of his father's dwelling off his feet. He had found me out. Accident had put him in the way of hearing his father's guilt pronounced by the lips of the wretch who executed the crime which his father had only meditated in evil dreams.

Claude Morel hunted me out in our house in London, and forced his way to my study in order to ask me for money. It was not his first attempt upon my purse after our joint crime. I had been pestered by letters from him, sometimes at long intervals, sometimes in rapid succession; but I had answered none of those letters; and now when he dared to force an entrance into my house I was rigid in my refusal of money. I knew what the word *chantage* means for a Frenchman of his temper; and that if I once opened my purse to him I should be his slave for ever. I was no coward in my relations with that scoundrel, although he threatened me with the one thing which I had to fear. He threatened to tell you the story of his crime, and how he took the first hint of it from my lips. He had kept the telegram sent from Reading on the morning of the murder—the telegram giving the hour of your husband's appointment; and he swore that if I denied him substantial help he would tell his story to you, and lay that telegram before you.

I bade him do his worst, strong in the assurance that he would do nothing to incriminate himself, and that he could not touch upon the subject of Robert Hatrell's death without jeopardising his own safety. Least of all did I believe that he would reveal himself to you as your husband's murderer. No; I felt that I had nothing to fear beyond personal annoyance from the existence of Claude Morel; yet the memories which the man pressed upon me were so hideous, his presence was so intolerable, that I would have given half my fortune to be rid of him for ever. It was as if my crime had taken a living shape and were dogging my steps. Most of all did I loathe his presence when he came upon me in my quiet study in this house—in the room where his crime and mine had first shaped itself in my disordered mind.

He had resolved to weary me out, I believe, and to that end he had taken a lodging at Henley. He appeared upon my pathway at all

hours and in the most unexpected places, but I
was rock.

We had several interviews before the one which
was fatal to my son's peace of mind, and which
parted father and son for ever.

On that particular morning Morel overtook me
in the lane near my cottage, and urged his
demands with a savage persistence, rendered
desperate, I suppose, by the disappointment of
hopes which he had entertained from the hour he
discovered that I was a rich man.

"You say that I knew you in London some
years ago," I said, "and that we had confidential
conversations together in this place, and that we
two together plotted the murder of my best
friend? You admit that you are a murderer,
and you ask me to believe that I am one, by
desire, and intention, and co-operation with you.
I choose to deny all your assertions; I choose to
say that I never saw your face till you forced
your way into my London house. If you persist
in the form of persecution which you have been
carrying on for the last six weeks it will be my

duty to hand you over to the police, and it will be *their* duty to discover whether you are a lunatic at large, or whether you are really the man you pretend to be, and the murderer of Robert Hatrell. In the latter case there must be people who can identify you. Some of those witnesses at the inquest who saw the murderer go in and out of the house in Denmark Street may still be within reach of a subpoena. If you annoy me any further in my own house or out of doors it will be needful for me take this step, and you may be sure I shall take it."

I had never been cooler than when I gave him this answer. I had weighed and measured the situation, and I did not believe he had power to harm me, be his malignity what it might. My crime might be even darker than his, but he could not touch my guilt with his little finger without his whole body being drawn into the meshes of the law. I knew that, and I could afford to laugh at his fury. To give him money, were it so much as a single sovereign, would be in somewise to acknowledge his claim and to establish a link between us. There should be no such link. And over and above this motive I abhorred the man, and his necessities had no power to touch my pity.

He could do me no harm, I thought; nor could he, but for the accident of my son's crossing the top of the lane while this man was with me, and having his attention attracted by the strangeness of the man's gestures as he talked to me. The angry flourish of his arm as he poured his rancour into my ear suggested a threat of personal violence, and my son followed us, in order to protect his father should there be need of his interference. Once within earshot Cyril stayed his footsteps and listened to the end of a savage recapitulation of those suggestions of mine which led to the scheme of the murder, and of the sending of the telegram that furnished the information which rendered the crime possible.

He, my son, heard the history of my sin, heard and believed. I stopped at the end of the lane and looked round. Cyril stood a few paces from me, deadly pale, looking at me in terrible silence. Morel turned and saw him stand there, almost at the same moment, and slunk aside.

"How dare you insult my father with your lunatic ravings?" cried Cyril, lifting his stick threateningly; "be off with you, fellow."

He pointed Londonwards with his stick, and Morel crept slowly along the dusty road, leaving me face to face with my son.

"You don't believe——" I began; but his face told me that he did believe Morel's story, and that nothing I could say would undo the mischief that scoundrel's tongue had done. The story of the telegram had condemned me in my son's eyes; and perhaps, too, my guilt was written upon my brow, had been written there from the beginning in characters that had deepened with the passage of time. Oh, God! how often, sitting among you all, within the sound of Daisy's innocent laughter, I have found the burden of my guilt so intolerable, that I have been tempted to cry my secret aloud and make an end of my long agony! And now I saw all the horror of it reflected in my son's agonised face as he told me that he could never be Daisy's husband, that the murderer's son must not marry the victim's daughter.

"Oh, how she would hate me," he cried, "if years after our marriage she found she had been entrapped into such a loathsome union!"

He told me that he should leave England at once, and for ever. He was not without pity for me, although my crime and the passion that prompted it lay beyond the region of his thoughts. To him such a character as mine was unthinkable.

He who could renounce love when honour urged him could not understand the love that makes light of honour, truth, friendship, all things for love's sake. His happier nature has never sounded *that* dark depth.

And so we parted. I wanted him at least to share my fortune. There was no taint at the source of this. If he were to begin a new life, I urged that he might as well begin it with independence and comfort; but he told me he could take nothing from me, and he was resolute in his refusal.

"I am young enough to make my own way in the world," he told me; "thews and sinews must have their value somewhere."

And so we parted, just touched ice-cold hands, and parted for ever.

THE END.

LONDON: PRINTED BY WILLIAM CLOWES AND SONS, LIMITED,
STAMFORD STREET AND CHARING CROSS.

www.ingramcontent.com/pod-product-compliance
Lightning Source LLC
Chambersburg PA
CBHW030640030726
47497CB00006B/1877